THE ISLAND OF DOCTOR MOREAU

H. G. WELLS (1866–1946) was born to lower middle-class parents in straitened circumstances in the Kentish market town of Bromley. He was apprenticed to a draper, a position he loathed, but won a scholarship to the Normal School of Science in Kensington, which had been recently established under the leadership of the eminent biologist T. H. Huxley. There he was trained to be amongst the first generation of school science teachers. He did not complete his degree, but did begin to write and edit a student journal. His brief career as a teacher was ended by illness, and he turned to science journalism and reviewing professionally. He finally published *The Time Machine* as his first book in 1895. This 'scientific romance' was enthusiastically received by leading critics and editors and Wells began a whirlwind writing career, often writing several books a year. By 1901 he had completed several of his most famous scientific romances, including *The Island of Dr Moreau* (1896), *The Invisible Man* (1897), *The War of the Worlds* (1898), and *The First Men in the Moon* (1901).

After his non-fiction speculations on the year 2000, *Anticipations* (1901), Wells became a leading social and political commentator. He wrote utopias, comic novels of lower middle-class life, and 'problem novels', often on controversial subjects, such as sexual freedom for women in *Ann Veronica* (1909). He was associated with the liberal-left Fabian Society, although scandalized respectable society with a string of affairs. He also alienated many literary figures, quarrelling with Henry James over the purpose of fiction. Modernists like Virginia Woolf and E. M. Forster despised his work and often defined their new style against his. Yet with *An Outline of History* (1919), his epic and controversial history of the world, Wells became a truly global figure. After the Great War, he campaigned for world government and in the 1930s visited both American and Soviet leaders to press for peaceful solutions. He lived long enough to see the atomic bomb, something he accurately predicted in *The World Set Free* (1914), used on Japan. One of his last books was called *Mind at the End of Its Tether* (1945).

DARRYL JONES is Professor of English at Trinity College Dublin, where he has taught since 1994. His publications include *Horror: A Thematic History in Fiction and Film* (2002) and *Jane Austen* (2004). He has edited *Horror Stories: Classic Tales from Hoffmann to Hodgson* (2014), M. R. James's *Collected Ghost Stories* (2013), and Arthur Conan Doyle's *Gothic Tales* (2016) for Oxford World's Classics.

OXFORD WORLD'S CLASSICS

For over 100 years Oxford World's Classics have brought readers closer to the world's great literature. Now with over 700 titles—from the 4,000-year-old myths of Mesopotamia to the twentieth century's greatest novels—the series makes available lesser-known as well as celebrated writing.

The pocket-sized hardbacks of the early years contained introductions by Virginia Woolf, T. S. Eliot, Graham Greene, and other literary figures which enriched the experience of reading. Today the series is recognized for its fine scholarship and reliability in texts that span world literature, drama and poetry, religion, philosophy and politics. Each edition includes perceptive commentary and essential background information to meet the changing needs of readers.

OXFORD WORLD'S CLASSICS

H. G. WELLS

The Island of Doctor Moreau

Edited with an Introduction and Notes by
DARRYL JONES

OXFORD
UNIVERSITY PRESS

OXFORD
UNIVERSITY PRESS

Great Clarendon Street, Oxford, OX2 6DP
United Kingdom

Oxford University Press is a department of the University of Oxford.
It furthers the University's objective of excellence in research, scholarship,
and education by publishing worldwide. Oxford is a registered trade mark of
Oxford University Press in the UK and in certain other countries

First published as an Oxford World's Classics paperback 2017

Impression: 2

Published in the United States of America by Oxford University Press
198 Madison Avenue, New York, NY 10016, United States of America

British Library Cataloguing in Publication Data

Data available

Library of Congress Control Number: 2016946806

ISBN 978–0–19–870266–5

Printed in Great Britain by
Clays Ltd, St Ives plc

ACKNOWLEDGEMENTS

I WOULD like to begin by thanking my editors at OUP. Judith Luna first suggested that I might be interested in this project, and made me into a textual editor, for better or for worse. Luciana O'Flaherty has been a model of patience and understanding during the often difficult process of getting this book ready for publication, and I cannot thank her enough.

I owe so many intellectual debts, many of which are also debts of friendship. The first is to Kate Hebblethwaite, for very many discussions during which she shared with me her deep research into the meaning of Victorian beastliness, and we shared our enthusiasm for H. G. Wells. Nick Daly, Deaglán Ó Donghaile, and Ailise Bulfin have long been inspiring interlocutors, in person and in print. As ever, conversations with Jarlath Killeen, the best of friends and colleagues, only showed me how little I know about the nineteenth century. Thanks also to Jenny Brown, Ruth Doherty, Dara Downey, Trish Ferguson, Laura Habbe, Miles Link, Bernice Murphy, Elizabeth McCarthy, Eve Patten, Conor Reid, and to all my students. Some of the work for this edition was made possible by research funding from Trinity College Dublin—I am grateful to Linda Hogan for understanding the importance of books.

Working on a book in which there is so much pain and suffering would not have been bearable without my wife, Margaret Robson, and my daughter, Morgan Jones.

CONTENTS

INTRODUCTION

Readers who are unfamiliar with the novel may prefer to treat the Introduction as an Afterword

It 'ought never to have been written'.[1] The *Review of Reviews*' hostile response to *The Island of Doctor Moreau*, H. G. Wells's third novel, published in April 1896, was by no means untypical. Just a year previously, the selfsame *Review of Reviews* had greeted the publication of Wells's debut novel, *The Time Machine*, as marking the arrival of 'a man of genius' upon the literary scene.[2] But now the widespread consensus was that the young author had gone too far—in exploring the outer limits of his undoubted talent and imagination, he had transgressed the boundaries of decency.

Unlike almost all of Wells's novels of the 1890s, *Moreau* had not first been published in serial form—because, a recent biographer suggests, its content was considered too extreme.[3] Indeed, Wells's letters from around this time are full of complaints that the novel was not even being properly marketed or distributed by its publisher, William Heinemann. Looking to broker a new publishing deal with J. M. Dent, Wells complained that Heinemann 'disappointed by funking the "Island" pitifully because the Chronicle slated it'.[4] Pretty much everyone, in fact, slated it. In *The Athenaeum*, the historian Basil Williams called it 'nauseating'.[5] *The Speaker* believed that *Moreau* marked a new low point for the novel as a literary form, offering as it did 'still lower depths of nastiness, and still cruder manifestations of imbecility' than anything seen hitherto.[6] Perhaps worst of all,

[1] Michael Sherborne, *H. G. Wells: Another Kind of Life* (London, 2010), 114.
[2] [Anon.], 'A Man of Genius', *Review of Reviews* 11 (March 1895), 263, in Patrick Parrinder (ed.), *H. G. Wells: The Critical Heritage* (London, 1972), 33. This notice was either written by the *Review of Reviews*'s founding editor, W. T. Stead, or by his assistant, Grant Richards: both would later take credit for having 'discovered' H. G. Wells.
[3] Sherborne, *Wells: Another Kind of Life*, 112.
[4] H. G. Wells to J. M. Dent (letter of 12 September 1896), in *The Correspondence of H. G. Wells*, i. *1880–1903*, ed. David C. Smith (London, 1998), 268.
[5] Basil Williams, unsigned review in *The Athenaeum* (9 May 1896), 615–16, in Parrinder (ed.), *Critical Heritage*, 51.
[6] Unsigned review, *The Speaker* 13 (18 April 1896), in Parrinder (ed.), *Critical Heritage*, 51.

Wells's colleague on the *Saturday Review*, the distinguished zoologist
Peter Chalmers Mitchell—later secretary of the Zoological Society
of London and biographer of Wells's scientific idol T. H. Huxley—
wrote a damning review of *Moreau*, claiming that the novel was
misleading and founded on scientific error—assertions which Wells
vigorously disputed.[7]

Delivering its *coup de grâce*, the *Review of Reviews* suggested that
the novel should be withdrawn from circulation[8]—which was, in effect,
Wells believed, what Heinemann had done. At around this time, he
wrote complainingly to the novelist Grant Allen that 'Publishers are
I think . . . the most stupid human beings. There is no publisher in
London . . . with the intelligence & originality to set fashions.'[9] 'I hope
you've read The Island of Doctor Moreau,' he wrote to his long-time
friend and correspondent Elizabeth Healey in the spring of 1896,
'and I do hope that you don't think [it] merely a festival of 'orrors.'[10]
On December 1896, Wells wrote plaintively to an unknown admirer
of the novel, 'I'm very glad to find anyone who thinks well of my
Moreau. The book was unlucky at the outset but I think it has the
vitality to live through its troubles. My warmest thanks to you for
backing my opinion. Voluntary appreciations such as yours are one of
the pleasant things in authorship.'[11] The publication and reception of
Moreau had clearly been a bruising experience for H. G. Wells.

In his second novel, *The Wonderful Visit* (1895), an Angel is acci-
dentally shot by an English vicar, and is forced to spend some time
recuperating in the Home Counties. This affords Wells the opportunity for a wide-ranging and gently trenchant satire on *fin-de-siècle*
England. At its close, having been shunned, mistreated, and victim-
ized by almost everyone he encounters, the Angel laments, 'Truly,
this is no world for an Angel. . . . It is a World of War, a World of Pain,
a World of Death.'[12] This bleak conclusion is typical of the early

---

[7] Chalmers Mitchell, *Saturday Review* 81 (11 April 1896), 308–9, in Parrinder (ed.),
Critical Heritage, 43–6. For Wells's response to Chalmers Mitchell, see Wells to the Editor,
Saturday Review (letter [undated, *c*.1 November 1896]), in *Correspondence*, i. 275–6.

[8] Sherborne, *Wells: Another Kind of Life*, 114.

[9] Wells to Grant Allen (letter [undated]), in *Correspondence*, i. 264–5.

[10] Wells to Elizabeth Healey (letter [undated, late spring 1896]), in *Correspondence*, i. 261.

[11] Wells to an unknown recipient (letter of 17 December 1896), in *Correspondence*, i.
279–80.

[12] Wells, *The Wonderful Visit*, in *The Works of H. G. Wells*, Atlantic Edition, i. *The Time
Machine, The Wonderful Visit, and Other Stories* (London, 1924), 269.

phase of Wells's fiction, which tends, as Steven McLean has argued, to be characterized by an outlook of 'extreme pessimism'.[13] *The Island of Doctor Moreau* takes the Angel's intuition further still, literalizing his metaphor of 'a World of Pain': 'It was as if all the pain in the world had found a voice' (p. 34), Prendick says on hearing the cries of the vivisected puma.

Saturated in pain and disgust, suffused with grotesque and often unbearable images of torture and bodily mutilation, *The Island of Doctor Moreau* is unquestionably an extreme novel. The issues it raises and the images it presents remain shocking. Wells was not altogether wrong to fear that it would be read as 'a festival of 'orrors'—it's the nearest he ever got, certainly in his long fiction, to writing straightforward horror. But *Moreau* is also a serious, and highly knowledgeable, philosophical engagement with Wells's times, with their climate of scientific openness and advancement, but also their anxieties about the ethical nature of scientific discoveries, and their implications for religion; with their speculations about the nature and origins of humanity; and with their often confused and anguished pronouncements on race and empire—pronouncements from which Wells himself, we shall see, was not immune. *The Island of Doctor Moreau* is, like all of Wells's best fiction, fundamentally a novel of ideas.

H. G. Wells was a trained scientist. In the 1880s he had studied Zoology in the Normal School of Science in London (now Imperial College) under the tutelage of the great Victorian evolutionary theorist T. H. Huxley. He was well aware of what was for him the intimate relationship between scientific discourse on the one hand and imaginative literature on the other. For Wells, at least, far from representing the irreconcilable 'Two Cultures' that C. P. Snow was famously to observe in the twentieth century, science and literature were both part of the same endeavour.[14] Thus, at the same time as he was beginning to make a name for himself as a novelist in the mid-1890s, he was also carving out a living and an identity as a prolific scientific essayist. An 1894 essay, 'Popularising Science', makes explicit Wells's ideas on the

---

[13] Steven McLean, *The Early Fiction of H. G. Wells: Fantasies of Science* (London, 2009), 39.
[14] 'The Two Cultures' was the title of the scientist-novelist C. P. Snow's influential 1959 Rede Lecture at Cambridge University, later published as *The Two Cultures and the Scientific Revolution* (Cambridge, 1959).

relationship between literature—and most particularly popular genre fiction—and the scientific method:

> The taste for good, inductive reasoning is very widely diffused; there is a keen pleasure in seeing a previously unexpected generalisation skilfully developed. . . . The fundamental principles that underlie such stories as Poe's 'Murders in the Rue Morgue', or Conan Doyle's 'Sherlock Holmes' series, are precisely those that should guide a scientific writer.[15]

Like Arthur Conan Doyle, in fact, and many other writers of their generation, Wells was lucky to be writing at a boom time for the publication of popular genre fiction. In the 1880s, Cassell began to publish a series of reasonably priced (1 shilling) single-volume novels, of which Robert Louis Stevenson's *Treasure Island* (1883) and H. Rider Haggard's *King Solomon's Mines* (1885) were notable, stunning successes.[16] The success of novels such as these, along with the contemporaneous decline of formerly all-powerful circulating libraries such as Mudie's, were the death knell for the great publishing vehicle for Victorian realism, the 'three-decker' novel, which had effectively vanished by the mid-1890s. A new, largely urban, relatively classless reading public emerged, with a taste for shorter, more spectacularly exciting fiction, fed by the one-volume novels, but also by the emergence of the *Strand Magazine* (1891) and a host of others, often specializing in short-form fiction.[17] Out of this publishing revolution emerged, in their recognizably modern forms, many of the great genres of twentieth-century popular fiction—the detective story, the horror story, the adventure story, the ghost story, and the science fiction story—or, to use Wells's own term, the scientific romance.

As well as being a combination of the scientific romance and horror story, *The Island of Doctor Moreau* very self-consciously partakes in another important literary subgenre. It is an island novel. Traditionally, this form uses its remote, isolated, exotic locations as vehicles for the examination of the nature of human society, or even of human nature itself. Thomas More's *Utopia*, Daniel Defoe's *Robinson Crusoe*, Jonathan

---

[15] Wells, 'Popularising Science', *Nature* 50 (July 1894), 301.

[16] See Peter Keating, *The Haunted Study: A Social History of the English Novel, 1875–1914* (London, 1989), 15–16. This passage on the literary marketplace of the late nineteenth century draws heavily on Keating's work.

[17] As Keating notes, the very concept of the 'short story' as it is understood today was formulated out of this climate; *Haunted Study*, 39 ff.

Swift's *Gulliver's Travels*, R. M. Ballantyne's *The Coral Island*, William Golding's *Lord of the Flies*, and many others all operate in this way. Even *Treasure Island*, the example chronologically nearest to Moreau, has interesting things to say about class to its implied readership of young boys. At a crucial stage in the novel, young Jim Hawkins has to decide whose side he is on: the exciting, dangerous, disreputable, working-class pirate crew of Long John Silver, or the respectable landowning gentry and bourgeoisie represented by Squire Trelawney and Dr Livesey. As a good Victorian, Jim casts his lot with the forces of order, dull but respectable, for whom effectively he works as a double agent.

If island fiction is fundamentally an intellectual form, then the message of *Moreau* is a very unsettling one. From the very start of the novel, we are made aware that something terrible is going on, some kind of violation. From Montgomery's ominous observation that 'there were spots of blood on the gunwale' (p. 10) of the dinghy from which Prendick is rescued onwards, the early part of the novel is full of images and utterances which break down stable categories of social life, suffusing the novel with a sense of dread, a sense that something inarticulable, perhaps unspeakable, is going on. In her classic work *Purity and Danger* (1966), the anthropologist Mary Douglas argues that pollution and taboo arise from the violation of the clear category distinctions through which social organization—and perhaps the human mind itself—is structured.[18] Straying into the interstices between these clear categories has tended to produce, Douglas argues, social or existential disorientation, revulsion, or disgust. It is on the border between the supposedly distinct categories of human and animal that *Moreau* situates itself, leaving its characters—and perhaps its readers (certainly many of its initial readers in 1896)—all at sea, profoundly shocked by what they encounter. What they encounter, there on Noble's Isle far out in the Pacific Ocean, is something of which they cannot (and should not) speak, for which their language has no signifiers. On first encountering one of the Beast Men, Prendick feels that 'In some indefinable way, the black face thus flashed upon me shocked me profoundly' (p. 13). Moreau himself acknowledges to Prendick that 'Our little establishment here contains a secret or so,

[18] Mary Douglas, *Purity and Danger: An Analysis of the Concepts of Pollution and Taboo* (London, 1966).

is a kind of Bluebeard's Chamber, in fact' (p. 28).[19] What is the nature of the violation, this terrible, shocking, unspeakable, secret thing? Why are Dr Moreau's activities so *wrong*?

Looking back on *Moreau* for the publication of the Atlantic Edition of his works in 1924, Wells observed that 'the influence of Swift is very apparent in it'.[20] Indeed, the coda to *Moreau* directly parallels that of *Gulliver's Travels*—just as Gulliver returns to England but—having been given a view of humanity at its most base and bestial—can now see only Yahoos, and feel only disgust, so Prendick, returning home at last, is revolted by what he sees: 'When I lived in London the horror was wellnigh insupportable. I could not get away from men' (p. 116). In his influential critical study *The Intellectuals and the Masses*, John Carey notes the particular appeal of writers such as Wells to a new and characteristic representative of Victorian modernity, the suburban commuter. The short form of much *fin-de-siècle* genre fiction, and its relative lack of formal and aesthetic complexity, made it ideal reading material for the commute to and from work in the city.[21] It is these people—Wells's own reading public—that really disgust Prendick:

weary pale workers go coughing by me, with tired eyes and eager paces like wounded deer dripping blood [. . .] Particularly nauseous were the blank expressionless faces of people in trains and omnibuses; they seemed no more my fellow-creatures than dead bodies would be, so that I did not dare to travel unless I was assured of being alone. (pp. 116–17)

Wells's fiction would soon find ingenious ways of doing away with these suburban commuters: when the Martians arrive to wreak their holocaust upon humanity in *The War of the Worlds* (1898), it is to the London suburbs that they come first.

The Island of Dr Moreau itself, Noble's Isle, is quite deliberately and precisely located on the novel's opening page. The *Lady Vain*, on which Edward Prendick is a passenger, is shipwrecked at 'latitude 1° s. and

[19] The most famous version of the folk tale of Bluebeard was published by Charles Perrault in 1697. Bluebeard is a serial wife-murderer who keeps the corpses of his victims locked in a secret chamber in his castle.

[20] Wells, 'Preface to Volume II', in *The Works of H. G. Wells*, Atlantic Edition, vol. ii, p. ix.

[21] John Carey, *The Intellectuals and the Masses: Pride and Prejudice among the Literary Intelligentsia, 1880–1939* (London, 1992), 46–70. For a full-length study of the significance of figures such as this, see Jonathan Wild, *The Rise of the Office Clerk in Literary Culture, 1880–1939* (London, 2006).

longitude 107 w.' (p. 3). This situates the action of the novel, and Noble's Isle itself, in the Pacific Ocean, a few hundred miles west of Ecuador. That is to say, Noble's Isle occupies the same imaginative territory that the Galapagos Islands do on a real map of the world.

'The natural history of this archipelago is very remarkable: it seems to be a little world within itself; the greater number of its inhabitants being found nowhere else.'[22] So wrote Charles Darwin in *The Voyage of the Beagle*, published in 1839. 'The voyage of the *Beagle*', Darwin was later to recall, 'has been by far the most important event in my life and has determined my whole career.'[23] HMS *Beagle*, with Darwin on board as a naturalist, visited the Galapagos in September and October 1835. Darwin's observations of the unique fauna of the islands, and particularly its many varieties of finches, had a very profound effect on his later thinking. The evolutionary biologist Stephen Jay Gould has warned against straightforwardly accepting the 'myth of the *Beagle*'— according to which, on setting foot on the Galapagos, the scales fell from Darwin's eyes, converting him instantly to an evolutionist— reminding us that 'Darwin entered and left the Galápagos as a creationist'.[24] Nevertheless this visit to the archipelago was the major formative event in the long process that led to the publication of *The Origin of Species* in 1859.

From the perspective of a modern evolutionary biologist, Gould writes of the Galapagos:

Isolated oceanic islands are the great natural laboratories of evolution. . . . Many features conspire to turn islands into crucibles for profound and rapid evolutionary change among their inhabitants: absence of competitors, ecological availability of unconventional niches, the small size of founding populations. Islands therefore become homes for bizarre versions of animals that may be stereotyped in continental situations throughout the world.[25]

Wells himself was completely aware of the evolutionary potential of islands, and—in yet another example of the interrelatedness of science

[22] Charles Darwin, *The Voyage of the Beagle*, ed. and introd. Janet Browne and Michael Neve (London, 1989), 269.   [23] Darwin, *Voyage of the Beagle*, 2.

[24] Stephen Jay Gould, 'Darwin at Sea—and the Virtues of Port', in *The Flamingo's Smile: Reflections in Natural History* (New York, 1985), 347, 355.

[25] Stephen Jay Gould, 'In an Evolutionary Crucible', *New York Review of Books* (20 November 1980), http://www.nybooks.com/articles/1980/11/20/in-an-evolutionary-crucible/.

and literature in his mind—had written a scientific essay on this very
subject a few months before the publication of *Moreau*. 'The Influence
of Islands on Variation', in fact, articulates a central scientific thesis of
the novel, that island life and human intervention are the two major
causes of species variation:

> When man has taken the wild things of the woods and domesticated them,
> he finds, even in the absence of conscious selection in his part, that the
> creatures gradually change in colour and shape and structure from their
> primitive form. . . . Island life offers a second case in which the abeyance of
> usual conditions of environment results in great variation. . . . The remot-
> est oceanic islands, indeed, contain practically no true natives; their popu-
> lation consists of creatures that may be blown to them on the wings of the
> wind, or wafted to them across measureless expanses of ocean. Having
> reached their isolated new homes, they vary abundantly. . . . Now the spe-
> cial point of this little essay is to suggest that isolation on islands has played
> a larger part in the evolution of animals and plants than is usually attrib-
> uted to it.[26]

Islands, Wells realized, could act not only as crucibles of evolution
but also as powerful reminders of the place of humanity in evolution,
and as a product of evolution. As with Gulliver and Prendick, island
encounters raise questions about the nature of humanity, and our
supposed place at the pinnacle of creation.

    This is exactly the territory Wells explores in his other island fic-
tion of the 1890s, the short story 'Æpyornis Island' (1894). Here, an
orchid-hunter is trapped on a desert island with an extinct flightless
bird, and soon finds himself in a desperate struggle for survival:
'I admit I felt small to see this blessed fossil lording it there. . . . A great,
gawky, out-of-date bird! And me a human being—heir of the ages
and all that.'[27] In the introduction to their collection of his scientific
writings, Robert Philmus and David Y. Hughes note that the 'repu-
diation of anthropocentricity' is central to Wells's vision, particularly
in the 1890s.[28] We see this vision radically in *The Time Machine*, where
humanity splits over time into two distinct subspecies, the Eloi and
the Morlocks, before disappearing altogether from the surface of the

---

[26] Wells, 'The Influence of Islands on Variation', *Saturday Review* 80 (17 August
1895), 204.   [27] Wells, 'Æpyornis Island', in *Works*, Atlantic Edition, i. 333.
[28] Wells, *Early Writings in Science and Science Fiction*, ed. Robert Philmus and David
Y. Hughes (Berkeley and Los Angeles, 1975), 15.

earth, whose last inhabitant at the end of time is some tentacular creature 'hopping fitfully about'.[29] In *The War of the Worlds* (1898), human dominance of the planet proves no match for superior Martian technology; we are saved only by the presence of Earth's primordial life-forms, the germs against which the Martians have no resistance.

'Æpyornis Island' was first published in the *Pall Mall Budget* on 27 December 1894. A few days earlier, Wells had published a scientific essay, 'The Rate of Change in Species' which mused on the slowness of human evolution, fundamentally unchanged since the Stone Age. The logic of this observation leads Wells to a bleak conclusion, which precisely anticipates the orchid-hunter's terminology in 'Æpyornis Island':

The true heirs of the future are the small, fecund and precocious creatures; those obscure, innumerable plastic species that die in myriads and yet do not diminish . . . No doubt man is lord of the earth to-day, but the lordship of the future is another matter. . . . No doubt he is heir of all the ages, but the herring, the frog, the Aphis, or the rabbit, it may be, is the residuary legatee.[30]

The 'hopping creature' that is *The Time Machine*'s residuary legatee to the ages may well be an evolved descendant of a frog, or perhaps a rabbit. The rabbits which Moreau has brought to Noble's Isle for a food supply make frequent cameo appearances throughout the novel, there in the background or middle distance—Wells rarely passes up an opportunity to remind us of their presence (I count about a dozen appearances in what is not in any case a long novel). Indeed, attentive readers will spot them on the novel's opening page, listed among the surviving fauna discovered on Noble's Isle when HMS *Scorpion* visits there in 1891, some four years after the action of the novel: 'A party of sailors then landed, but found nothing living thereon except certain curious white moths, some hogs and rabbits, and some rather peculiar rats' (p. 3).

It is difficult to overestimate the psychic shock which the publication of *The Origin of Species* caused to Victorian society in 1859. It brought about a profound revolution—a paradigm shift—in scientific, social, cultural, and religious thinking. The mid-Victorian 'crisis

[29] Wells, *The Time Machine*, in *Works*, Atlantic Edition, i. 111.
[30] Wells, 'The Rate of Change in Species', *Saturday Review* 78 (15 December 1894), 666.

of faith' is directly attributable to the publication of this book.[31] Two of the most characteristic, and diametrically opposed, features of British cultural life in the second half of the nineteenth century, scientific materialism and spiritualism, can both be traced back to Darwinism and its implications.[32] As Gillian Beer writes, 'In its imaginative consequences for science, literature, society and feeling, *The Origin of Species* is one of the most extraordinary examples of a work which included more than the maker of it at the time knew, despite all that he *did* know.'[33] After Darwin, the concept of evolution, in all its facets, obsessed Victorian intellectual and social life.[34]

The dominant intellectual figure in the young H. G. Wells's life was the man who taught him Elementary Biology and Zoology at the Normal School of Science: the great Victorian naturalist and controversialist T. H. Huxley. More than any one figure except for Darwin himself, Huxley, the very embodiment of scientific materialism, exemplified the intellectual spirit of the age. Looking back in his *Experiment in Autobiography* (1934), Wells, now approaching 70, recalled the intellectual exhilaration of his student days: 'I was under the shadow of Huxley, the acutest observer, the ablest generalizer, the great teacher, the most lucid and valiant of controversialists. . . . That year I spent in Huxley's class, was beyond all question, the most educational year of my life.'[35] Wells knew that he was in the presence of a giant, one step away from Darwin himself:

These two were very great men. They thought boldly, carefully and simply, they spoke and wrote fearlessly and plainly, they lived modestly and decently,

---

[31] For the Victorian 'crisis of faith', see, for example, Elisabeth Jay, *Faith and Doubt in Victorian Britain* (London, 1986); Richard J. Helmstadter and Bernard Lightman (eds.), *Victorian Faith in Crisis: Essays on Continuity and Change in 19th-century Religious Belief* (Palo Alto, Calif., 1991).

[32] For scientific materialism (of scientific naturalism), see, for example, Gowan Dawson and Bernard Lightman (eds.), *Victorian Scientific Naturalism: Community, Identity, Continuity* (Chicago, 2014). For Victorian spiritualism, see, for example, Janet Oppenheim, *The Other World: Spiritualism and Psychical Research in England, 1850–1914* (Cambridge, 1988). For a study which brilliantly draws out the connections between the two, see Roger Luckhurst, *The Invention of Telepathy, 1870–1901* (Oxford, 2002), 9–59.

[33] Gillian Beer, *Darwin's Plots: Evolutionary Narrative in Darwin, George Eliot, and Nineteenth-Century Fiction* (3rd edn., Cambridge, 2009), 2.

[34] See J. W. Burrow, *Evolution and Society: A Study in Victorian Social Theory* (Cambridge, 1966).

[35] Wells, *Experiment in Autobiography: Discoveries and Conclusions of a Very Ordinary Brain (Since 1866)* (New York, 1934), 159, 161.

they were mighty intellectual liberators. . . . Darwin and Huxley, in their place and measure, belong to the same aristocracy as Plato and Aristotle and Galileo, and they will ultimately dominate the priestly and orthodox mind as surely, because there is a response, however reluctant, masked and stifled, in every human soul to rightness and firmly stated truth.[36]

Although *The Origin of Species* itself had nothing explicit to say about human evolution, its implications were obvious—so obvious, in fact, that Darwin himself was to return openly to the issue of human evolution in *The Descent of Man* (1871), which set out 'to consider, firstly, whether man, like every other species, is descended from some pre-existing form; secondly, the manner of his development; and thirdly, the value of the difference between the so-called races of man'.[37] It is precisely these implications which underlay the famous exchange between Huxley and Bishop Samuel Wilberforce in a debate on evolution which took place in the Oxford University Museum of Natural History on 30 June 1860. Wilberforce, a noted orator, denounced evolution, and reportedly asked Huxley 'with a smiling insolence . . . was it through his grandfather or his grandmother that he claimed descent from a monkey?' Huxley, according to his own account at least, then turned to his neighbour Sir Benjamin Brodie and exclaimed, 'The Lord hath delivered him into my hands!' He then told Wilberforce that 'He was not ashamed to have a monkey for an ancestor; but he would be ashamed to be connected with a man who used great gifts to obscure the truth.'[38] Uproar ensued: 'One lady fainted and had to be carried out,' according to a witness, while Robert FitzRoy, formerly captain of the *Beagle* and now an admiral, brandished a Bible above his head, declaiming, 'the Book, the Book'.[39] Wells certainly recognized the shocking, blasphemous potential in human evolution and shared ancestry with the animals, as we shall see.

---

[36] Wells, *Experiment in Autobiography*, 162–3.

[37] Darwin, *The Descent of Man*, ed. and introd. James Moore and Adrian Desmond (London, 2004), 18.

[38] Leonard Huxley, *Life and Letters of Thomas Henry Huxley* (London, 1980), i. 265–7. Since no full contemporary account exists of this formative event in the history of Victorian science, and since the received version relied heavily on Huxley's own reminiscences of some decades later, Stephen Jay Gould has argued that we should treat his account with some caution: it was not understood, at least by witnesses, as the crushing blow to creationism that it has since become: see Gould, 'Knight Takes Bishop?', in *Bully for Brontosaurus: Reflections in Natural History* (London, 2001), 385–401.

[39] *Life and Letters of Thomas Henry Huxley*, 267; Gould, 'Darwin at Sea', 358.

The Island of Doctor Moreau is highly unusual for a number of reasons, but not least because it is largely populated by characters who are trained biologists: 'As it happens,' Moreau tells Prendick, ominously, 'we are biologists here. This is a biological station—of a sort' (p. 26). Prendick is effectively a counterpart for Wells in the novel, having 'spent some years at the Royal College of Science, and [. . .] done some research in biology under Huxley' (p. 26). Montgomery has a similar background: 'I did my Biology at University College' (p. 11), he tells Prendick. Moreau himself had been 'a prominent and masterful physiologist, well known in scientific circles' (p. 30). This raises a troubling question: why should Wells, whose essays of the period work tirelessly to promote scientific understanding among the reading public, have written a novel which views scientific advancement with such horror and disgust? *Moreau* is, in fact, a classic example of the major popular cultural discourse of 'mad science', which is typically fearful, intellectually conservative, and turning on a popular mistrust of scientists and their activities as inimical to humane morality.[40] As the astronomer Carl Sagan has written:

The technological perils that science serves up, its implicit challenge to received wisdom, and its perceived difficulty, are all reasons for some people to mistrust and avoid it. There's a reason people are nervous about science and technology. And so the image of the mad scientist haunts our world—down to the white-coated loonies of Saturday morning children's TV and the plethora of Faustian bargains in popular culture, from the eponymous Dr Faustus himself to Dr Frankenstein, Dr Strangelove, and *Jurassic Park*.

But we can't simply conclude that science puts too much power into the hands of morally-feeble technologists or corrupt, power-crazed politicians and so decide to get rid of it.[41]

Sagan's conclusion is one which Wells himself would surely have endorsed. As John Carey has pointed out, Wells the novelist and Wells the social and scientific theorist often seem to be pulling in two

[40] Much has been written on popular cultural mad science: see, for example, Roslynn D. Haynes, *From Faust to Strangelove: Representations of the Scientist in Western Literature* (Baltimore, 1994); David J. Skal, *Screams of Reason: Mad Science and Modern Culture* (New York, 1988); Christopher Frayling, *Mad, Bad and Dangerous? The Scientist and the Cinema* (London, 2005).

[41] Carl Sagan, *The Demon-Haunted World: Science as a Candle in the Dark* (London, 1997), 14.

contrary directions, 'nearly always in two minds', resulting in 'H. G. Wells against H. G. Wells'.[42] This should not surprise us: writers are often at their most fascinating and stimulating when they are divided or contradictory, and fiction often suffers badly when it is made to articulate clear-cut ideological positions.

We know that Wells considered much of what animates Moreau himself to be valuable science. Moreau's exploration of the permeable boundary between human and animal is an extrapolation of Darwinian natural selection. In 1863, Huxley himself had explored the same boundaries in *Man's Place in Nature*. This important work contains an extended morphological analysis of the great apes, whose conclusions closely anticipate some of the themes of *Moreau*. *Man's Place in Nature*, Huxley writes, is 'an inquiry into the nature and closeness of the ties which connect him [man] with those singular creatures', the apes:

Brought face to face with these blurred copies of himself, the least thoughtful man is conscious of a certain shock, due perhaps not so much to disgust at the aspect of what looks like an insulting caricature, as to the awakening of a sudden and profound mistrust of time-honoured theories and strongly-rooted prejudices regarding his own position in nature. . . . Without question, the mode of origin and the early stages of the development of man are identical with those of the animals immediately below him in the scale . . . [W]ithout doubt, in these respects, he is far nearer the Apes, than the Apes are to the Dog.[43]

Similarly, Prendick's revulsion towards the Beast Men is in part the shock of recognition. Encountering the Ape Man, he acknowledges some form of kinship, 'I did not feel the same repugnance towards this creature that I had experienced in my encounters with the other Beast Men [. . .] He was a man, then' (p. 48).

Furthermore, in making the Beast Men talk—in one case with an 'English accent [which] was strangely good' (p. 52)—the novel directs its energies at one of the central criticisms of the Victorian anti-Darwinist movement, the uniquely human status of language. Moreau explains that 'the great difference between man and monkey is in the larynx [. . .] in the incapacity to frame delicately different sound-symbols by which thought could be sustained' (p. 64). Attempts since

---

[42] Carey, *The Intellectuals and the Masses*, 135.

[43] Thomas Henry Huxley, 'Man's Place in Nature', in *Collected Essays*, vii. *Man's Place in Nature and Other Anthropological Essays* (London, 1906), 80, 89–90.

the Enlightenment by Lord Monboddo and others to teach apes to speak had invariably failed.[44] In a series of lectures in 1861 explicitly attacking Darwinian evolution, the great philologist and mythographer Max Müller asserted that 'the one great barrier between the brute and man is *Language*. Man speaks, and no brute has ever uttered a word. Language is our Rubicon, and no brute dares cross it.'[45] In crossing this Rubicon, Moreau is asserting the relatedness of man and beast.

Not only does Moreau's work echo that of Huxley, it also draws directly on Wells's own scientific thinking. 'These creatures you have seen', Moreau tells Prendick, 'are animals carven and wrought into new shapes. To that—to the study of the plasticity of living forms— my life has been devoted' (p. 63). Moreau's own account of his work, in the chapter 'Doctor Moreau Explains' (p. 62), draws, often verbatim, on Wells's own 1895 essay 'The Limits of Individual Plasticity'. The justificatory examples and allusions which Moreau offers—to the pioneering grafting experiments of John Hunter, to Victor Hugo's *L'Homme qui rit*—are the same ones which Wells himself had offered in his essay. Wells concludes his essay with a proposition as shocking as anything in *The Island of Doctor Moreau*:

we may imagine as possible in the future, operators armed with antiseptic surgery and a growing perfection of the knowledge of the laws of growth, taking living creatures and moulding them into the most amazing forms; it may be, even reviving the monsters of mythology, realizing the fantasies of the taxidermist, his mermaids, and what-not, in flesh and blood.[46]

Part of what Moreau does is to put into practice, at least fictively, Wells's own speculative fantasies. In the 'Note' which he appended to the first edition, Wells affirms that 'the manufacture of monsters— and perhaps even of *quasi*-human monsters—is within the possibilities of vivisection' (p. 118).

The novel, then, is written from an intimate knowledge of biological theory, and to a certain extent presupposes some of the same knowledge in its readership. This is important, because the novel shows

[44] See Michael Newton, *Savage Girls and Wild Boys: A History of Feral Children* (London, 2002), 53–97.

[45] F. Max Müller, *Lectures on the Science of Language, Delivered at the Royal Institution of Great Britain in April, May, and June 1861* (London, 1862), in Christine Ferguson, *Language, Science and Popular Fiction in the Victorian Fin-de-Siècle* (London, 2006), 1. This passage draws heavily on Ferguson's illuminating study.

[46] Wells, 'The Limits of Individual Plasticity', *Saturday Review* 79 (19 January 1895), 90.

that Dr Moreau himself is anything but an orthodox Darwinian. Indeed, part of the horror of the novel arises from his own refusal to accept the strictures of Darwinian evolution, which required the vast time-frames established by the early nineteenth-century formulation of geological 'deep time' in works such as Charles Lyell's *Principles of Geology* (1833), which was a major influence on the intellectual development of Darwin himself.[47] Wells graduated in January 1891, earning the degree of Bachelor of Science with first-class honours in Zoology and second-class in Geology.[48] He understood the relationship between the two fields, and the implications of geological discoveries for natural selection. In his attempts to intervene directly and immediately in the evolutionary process, rather than shaping and guiding its development across many generations, Moreau's problem is that he is practising bad science, or adhering to an outmoded theory of evolution. He is not a Darwinian, but a Lamarckian. The evolutionary theories of the French naturalist Jean-Baptiste Lamarck (1744–1829) rested on the principle of the inheritance of acquired characteristics, a principle discredited by Darwinian natural selection, and later comprehensively disproven by Mendelian genetics.[49] Although Lamarck himself is not named in the novel, Montgomery makes direct reference to Moreau's Lamarckian aims when he tells Prendick that, in the offspring of the Beast People, 'There was no evidence of the inheritance of acquired human characteristics' (p. 72); 'but somehow', Moreau acknowledges, with frustration, 'the stubborn beast flesh grows, day by day, back again' (p. 68).

Moreau's evolutionary principles, then, are pre-Darwinian, and therefore run counter to the theory of natural selection. But they also put him in avowed opposition to T. H. Huxley. The novel, we have seen, presents Moreau's activities in terms of a profound violation, something shocking and unspeakable. When Prendick confronts him on this, protesting that his vivisected puma is 'an abomination', Moreau counters in archetypal mad science terms: 'To this day I have never troubled about the ethics of the matter. The study of Nature

---

[47] For an important account of the influence of geological 'deep time' upon nineteenth-century thought, and upon Darwin himself, see Michael Freeman, *Victorians and the Prehistoric: Tracks to a Lost World* (New Haven, 2004).

[48] Sherborne, *Wells: Another Kind of Life*, 76.

[49] For Lamarck, see Peter J. Bowler, *Evolution: The History of an Idea* (25th anniversary edn., Berkeley and Los Angeles, 2009), 86–94.

makes man at last as remorseless as Nature' (p. 66). In 1893, just three years before the publication of *Moreau*, Huxley himself was sufficiently 'troubled about the ethics of the matter' to have written a major work on the subject, *Evolution and Ethics*. Huxley's last significant public statement, this was a very high-profile work, with its origins in the 1893 Romanes Lecture at Oxford University, 'the major public lecture of the University. A most distinguished figure from the arts, science or literature is invited by special invitation of the Vice Chancellor.'[50] (Huxley was only the second Romanes lecturer; the first, in 1892, was Prime Minister William Ewart Gladstone.) Huxley used the platform of the Romanes Lecture to denounce the social Darwinist movement, most closely associated with Herbert Spencer, whose *Principles of Biology* (1864) coined the phrase most associated with social Darwinism, 'the survival of the fittest', which Spencer understood as synonymous with 'natural selection'.[51] In *Evolution and Ethics*, Huxley argues that the application of natural selection to human society was based firstly on a misunderstanding of what evolutionary biology means by 'fitness':

I suspect that this fallacy has arisen out of the unfortunate ambiguity of the phrase 'survival of the fittest.' 'Fittest' has a connotation of 'best'; and about 'best' there hangs a moral flavour. In cosmic nature, however, what is 'fittest' depends only on conditions.[52]

Ethical science, Huxley asserts, turning Spencer's dictum on its head, 'is directed, not so much to the survival of the fittest as to the fitting of as many as possible to survive. It repudiates the gladiatorial theory of existence.'[53] In becoming 'as remorseless as Nature', then, *Moreau* has learned the wrong lesson from scientific progress, which has developed civilized, altruistic values as a means of countering the remorselessness of Nature: 'Let us understand,' Huxley concludes, 'once and for all, that the ethical progress of society depends, not on imitating the cosmic process, still less in running away from it, but in combating it.'[54]

---

[50] 'Romanes Lecture', http://www.ox.ac.uk/news-and-events/The-University-Year/romanes-lecture.

[51] Herbert Spencer, *The Principles of Biology* (London, 1865), 444–5.

[52] Huxley, 'Evolution and Ethics', in *Collected Essays*, ix. *Evolution & Ethics and Other Essays* (London, 1906), 80.   [53] Huxley, 'Evolution and Ethics', 82.

[54] Huxley, 'Evolution and Ethics', 83.

Moreau combats Nature in quite another way. 'What could it mean?' Prendick asks himself after hearing Moreau's narrative; 'A locked enclosure on a lonely island, a notorious vivisector, and these crippled and distorted men?' (p. 31). Prendick remembers having read 'The Moreau Horrors', the title of 'a little buff-coloured pamphlet' which described events which took place 'ten years' before the action of the novel—that is, in around 1877. Moreau, he recalls, had been

a prominent and masterful physiologist, well known in scientific circles for his extraordinary imagination and his brutal directness in discussion. [. . .] He had published some very astonishing facts in connection with the transfusion of blood, and, in addition, was known to be doing valuable work on morbid growths. Then suddenly his career was closed. [. . . The] gruesome pamphlet became notorious. On the day of its publication, a wretched dog, flayed and otherwise mutilated, escaped from Moreau's house. (p. 31)

It is significant that 'The Moreau Horrors' belong initially to the 1870s, a key decade in the history of British physiology, and consequently the major decade for public debate on the ethics of vivisection.

The rise of experimental physiology as a separate academic medical discipline in the early nineteenth century brought with it serious concerns about the ethics of animal experimentation. In Britain, this led to the passing of Martin's Act of 1822, which forbade cruelty to large domestic animals, but not initially to cats and dogs.

In 1824, the French physiologist François Magendie visited London, where he gave a series of public lectures and vivisection demonstrations. The public shock and outcry which these events caused contributed directly to the foundation later that year of the Royal Society for the Prevention of Cruelty to Animals, whose first prospectus maintained 'that Providence cannot intend that the secrets of Nature should be discovered by means of cruelty'.[55] The introduction of anaesthesia to surgery in 1847, in the form of ether, brought an added dimension to the vivisection debates, and one which is clearly significant for *The Island of Doctor Moreau*, which relies so heavily for its effects on repeated and vivid accounts of pain and suffering. The guidelines for the 1871

---

[55] Richard D. French, *Antivivisection and Medical Science in Victorian Society* (Princeton, 1975), 28. Initially the Society for the Prevention of Cruelty to Animals, the RSPCA was granted royal status by Queen Victoria in 1840. This passage draws heavily on French's invaluable work.

report of the General Council of the British Association for the Advancement of Science required the use of anaesthetic for animal experiments, which were only to be carried out in laboratories 'under proper regulations'.[56]

The rumbling controversy over vivisection came to a head in August 1874, when the French physiologist Eugene Magnan gave a lecture and vivisection demonstration to a meeting of the British Medical Association in Norwich. This is the event which, in part, underlies 'The Moreau Horrors' (his French name is a distant echo of Magnan, and perhaps even of Magendie), which recalls some of its details. To the dismay of some members of the audience, including some senior medical figures, Magnan started to experiment on two dogs. Joliffe Tufnell, the president of the Royal College Surgeons in Ireland, interceded and cut the restraints of one of the dogs, and the poor beast was left staggering around the auditorium. The authorities were called, and the meeting broke up in disarray. The RSPCA brought a case against Magnan (who had fled to France) under Martin's Act.[57]

Darwin and Huxley both became involved in the vivisection debates of the 1870s, both asserting the necessity of experimental vivisection. The RSPCA, too, believed that vivisection should be permissible under certain tightly-controlled circumstances. It was the RSPCA's perceived lack of militancy that led to the establishment of a number of anti-vivisection societies in the 1870s, most notably Frances Power Cobbe's Victoria Street Society (formed in 1875, and later to become the British Anti-Vivisection Society). As a response to public pressure, the Royal Commission on Vivisection was established in 1875, with Huxley as a member. Its report in 1876 led directly to the Cruelty to Animals Act of the same year. It is for breaking the law by violating this Act that Moreau 'had to leave England. [. . .] The doctor was simply howled out of the country' (p. 31).

Of all the evidence given to the Royal Commission, the most sensational was that of Emanuel Klein, lecturer in Histology at St Bartholomew's Hospital. Huxley, the great advocate of ethical science, wrote in evident dismay to Darwin:

I am told that he openly professed the most entire indifference to animal suffering, and said he only gave anaesthetics to keep the animals quiet!

---

[56] French, *Antivivisection*, 45.   [57] French, *Antivivisection*, 55–6.

I declare to you I did not believe the man lived who was such an unmitigated cynical brute as to profess and act upon such principles, and I would willingly agree to any law which would send him to the treadmill. . . . He has done more mischief than all the fanatics put together.

I am utterly disgusted with the whole business.[58]

Klein's seemingly sadistic testimony was seized upon by the press. As Coral Lansbury notes in her account of the cultural significance of vivisection, more than any other episode it is Klein's testimony that creates in the popular imagination 'the figure of the archivivisector'.[59] The archivivisector—brilliant, often foreign, 'never troubled about the ethics of the matter'—is a recurring villain in late nineteenth-century popular fiction, as exemplified by the sinister, dog-flaying, paedophiliac Dr Benjulia in Wilkie Collins's *Heart and Science* (1883). Dr Moreau is the most notorious fictional vivisector of them all, and—bad reviews notwithstanding—the publication of Wells's novel seems to have inaugurated a small flurry of vivisection novels in the following years, including Sarah Grand's *The Beth Book* (1897), Barry Pain's *The Octave of Claudius* (1897), and Florence Marryat's *The Blood of the Vampire* (1897). In 1895, the year before the publication of *Moreau*, the Anglo-Australian novelist Guy Boothby published *A Bid for Fortune; or Dr Nikola's Vendetta*, the first in a series of five bestselling novels featuring a dazzlingly evil mesmerist and vivisector. The debates of the 1870s had not gone away.

Pain—extreme, prolonged agony—is fundamental to Moreau's practice. It is not, as in Klein's testimony, a perhaps unpleasant but necessary by-product of scientific discovery. The infliction of pain is at the very heart of what Moreau is trying to achieve: 'But I will conquer yet. Each time I dip a living creature into the bath of burning pain I say, This time I will burn out all the animal, this time I will make a rational creature of my own' (p. 69). What this means is that Moreau is not—or not primarily—a scientist at all. He is a theologian. 'We are on different platforms,' he tells Prendick; 'You are a materialist. [. . .] I am a religious man [. . .] as every sane man must

[58] Huxley, *Life and Letters*, ii. 171–2.

[59] Coral Lansbury, *The Old Brown Dog: Women, Workers and Vivisection in Edwardian England* (Madison, 1985), 130.

be' (pp. 65, 66). This interpretation is borne out by Wells's own description of *Moreau* as 'a theological grotesque'.[60]

Some of *Moreau*'s early reviews recognized the novel's blasphemous overtones. The anonymous reviewer of the Anglican weekly *The Guardian* precisely identified the novel's queasy dynamic: 'Sometimes one is inclined to think the intention of the author has been to satirise and rebuke the presumption of science; at other times his object seems to be to parody the work of the Creator of the human race, and cast contempt upon the dealings of God with His creatures.'[61] Strongly implicit in the subtitle of Mary Shelley's *Frankenstein, or the Modern Prometheus* (1818), the foundational text of modern mad science, the trope of the scientist 'playing God', usurping the role of the divine creature, recurs across the nineteenth and twentieth centuries, and has found a particular home in the cinema. It is a clear response to the climate of religious anxiety which accompanied scientific naturalism, and which, as we have seen, was intensified by the publication of *The Origin of Species*. In *The Island of Lost Souls*, the celebrated 1932 Paramount Pictures adaptation of *Moreau*, Dr Moreau (famously portrayed by Charles Laughton) asks Edward Parker (Richard Arlen) whether he knows 'what it feels like to be God'—the film was banned outright in Britain for twenty-five years as a direct result of its perceived blasphemy.[62]

Moreau keeps 'the stubborn beast flesh' in check by means of 'the Law', a litany imposed upon the Beast Folk in what is a clear grotesque of religious ritual, and which Moreau himself claims has its origins in the work of Kanaka missionaries. In its cadences and interdicts, the Law is a parodic version of the Ten Commandments. In formulating the Law, Wells recognizes one of the major discoveries of nineteenth-century anthropology, one which was to have a significant effect on the twentieth-century master narrative of Freudian psychoanalysis. The behaviour of the Beast Folk is regulated by a system of

[60] Wells, 'Preface to Volume II', *Works*, Atlantic Edition, vol. ii, p. ix.

[61] Unsigned review, *The Guardian*, 3 June 1896, 371, in Parrinder (ed.), *Critical Heritage*, 53 (the weekly *Guardian*, not to be confused with the *Manchester Guardian*, was at the time the leading newspaper of the Church of England). Wells himself thought that 'The *Guardian* critic seemed to be the only one who read it aright, and who therefore succeeded in giving a really intelligent notice of it': Parrinder, (ed.), *Critical Heritage*, 52.

[62] See Darryl Jones, *Horror: A Thematic History in Fiction and Film* (London, 2002), 51–2, for an account of cinematic mad scientists 'playing God'.

taboos. J. G. Frazer's *The Golden Bough* is one of the great systematiz-ing works of the Victorian imagination, and a foundational text for the discipline of anthropology. Its third volume, which appeared in 1911, is entitled *Taboo and the Perils of the Soul*.[63] This in turn heavily informed the work of Sigmund Freud, most particularly *Totem and Taboo* (1913).[64] Nineteenth-century anthropological discourse was an intellectual endeavour very clearly linked to the geopolitical practice of imperialism. From the publication in 1871 of E. B. Tylor's land-mark 2-volume study *Primitive Culture*, anthropology was heavily invested in analysing what Claude Lévi-Strauss called, in the title of his own classic study, *The Savage Mind*.[65]

Recurrent across human societies is the taboo against 'unclean eating', and most specifically cannibalism. As Jennifer Brown notes in her brilliant study *Cannibalism in Literature and Film*, for some mod-ern anthropologists, the notion of cannibalism as a widespread prac-tice is merely 'a racist myth', a perpetuation of imperial stereotypes: the nineteenth-century European explorers, missionaries, and colo-nial administrators whose encounters provided much of the anthropo-logical data, merely recorded what they expected to find—uncivilized, subhuman brutes.[66] Cannibalism, according to this reading, is part of a widepread cultural-imperial discourse of Orientalism: it might, in other words, tell us more about our own society than that of the 'savages'.[67] While Prendick certainly finds subhuman brutes on Noble's Isle, it may well be the case that he himself is the cannibal. The novel opens as a classic narrative of shipwreck and castaway, and so carries overtones of *The Tempest* and *Robinson Crusoe*, both narratives with cannibalistic elements, and of Edgar Allan Poe's spectacularly canni-balistic novel *The Narrative of Arthur Gordon Pym of Nantucket* (1838).

[63] J. G. Frazer, *The Golden Bough*, iii. *Taboo and the Perils of the Soul* (London, 1911).

[64] Sigmund Freud, *Totem and Taboo: Some Points of Agreement between the Mental Lives of Savages and Neurotics*, trans. James Strachey (London, 1950).

[65] Edward B. Tylor, *Primitive Culture*, 2 vols. (London, 1871); Claude Lévi-Strauss, *The Savage Mind* (trans. of *La Pensée sauvage*) (London, 1966).

[66] Jennifer Brown, *Cannibalism in Literature and Film* (London, 2013), 4. See most particularly here William Arens, *The Man-Eating Myth: Anthropology and Anthropophagy* (Oxford, 1979). Arens subsequently modified his position in 'Rethinking Anthropophagy', in Frances Barker, Peter Hulme, and Margaret Iversen (eds.), *Cannibalism and the Colonial World* (Cambridge, 1998), 39–62.

[67] In making this point, I am clearly indebted to Edward W. Said, *Orientalism* (London, 1978), albeit that Said has nothing directly to say about cannibalism in this book.

In 1884, the British yacht *Mignonette* was sunk in the South Atlantic. The three crewmen who survived, including the ship's captain, did so by killing and eating the cabin boy, Richard Parker. The case of the *Mignonette* resulted in a high-profile trial in 1884.[68] (By a ghoulish coincidence, the cannibalized cabin boy in Poe's novel was also called Richard Parker. This is probably why Prendick's surname is changed to Parker in *The Island of Lost Souls,* and certainly why Yann Martel has a tiger called Richard Parker in his novel of castaways and cannibalism, *Life of Pi.*) Like the *Mignonette*'s crew, Prendick and his fellow castaways initially draw lots with a view to eating the loser. Although Prendick avers that this does not come to pass, his narrative is nevertheless embedded within a history of cannibalism. The sinking of the *Lady Vain* 'has become almost as well known as the far more terrible *Medusa* case' (p. 7). This was the most famous instance of nineteenth-century shipwreck and cannibalism, immortalized in an 1819 painting by Théodore Géricault: the survivors of the raft of the French frigate *Méduse,* which sunk in the Atlantic in 1810, resorted to cannibalism and murder in order to stay alive. When Prendick is rescued from the dinghy, he is given a drink: 'a dose of some scarlet stuff, iced. It tasted like blood' (p. 10). He is an unclean-eater. 'This ship ain't for beasts and cannibals', the captain of the *Ipecacuanha* asserts. We know who the beasts are, and who the cannibals.

If, as Moreau endeavours to demonstrate, beasts can become men, then the corollary is also true: men can become beasts. One of the most troubling implications of Darwinian natural selection for many was its insistence on monogenetic evolution—descent from a single, common source. One response to this was nineteenth-century racial theory, which in turn rested on the concept of polygeny—that is, the theory of multiple origins—which posited that the different races of humanity evolved separately from one another.[69] The white and black 'races' shared no commonality: this could evidently be used as a justification for slavery, or for violent imperial conquest. The craniometrist Samuel George Morton attempted to 'prove' by the measurement of skull capacities the greater cranial power of 'the Caucasian race'.[70]

---

[68] See Neil Hanson, *The Custom of the Sea: The Story that Changed British Law* (New York, 1999).

[69] For an account of nineteenth-century racial theory, on which I draw here, see Stephen Jay Gould, *The Mismeasure of Man* (London, 1984).

[70] Gould, *Mismeasure of Man*, 82–101.

Drawing on Morton's findings, the influential *Types of Mankind* by Josiah C. Nott and George R. Gliddon worked hard to try to establish commonalities between indigenous Africans and apes, who were therefore clearly associated with one another, but not with Caucasians.[71] Darwin himself explicitly criticizes Nott and Gliddon several times in *The Descent of Man*, and rejects pologeny as 'a hopeless endeavour', because 'all the races of man are descended from a single primitive stock'.[72] Wells was completely aware of this, and Moreau's experiments are strongly inflected with the language of polygenetic racial theory, and so again deviate from classical Darwinism. 'I thought him a fair specimen of the negroid type' (p. 67), Moreau says of his first creation, a gorilla man, while the Satyr man has a 'face ovine in expression—like the coarser Hebrew type' (p. 76).

Wells knew that Moreau was a proponent of spurious racial theory, and yet five years later, in the conclusion of *Anticipations* (1901), his first full-length work of social theory, he made his most notorious statement on race:

And for the rest—those swarms of black and brown and yellow people who do not come into the new needs of efficiency?

Well, the world is a world, not a charitable institution, and I take it they will have to go. The whole tenor and meaning of the world, as I see it, is that they have to go. So far as they fail to develop sane, vigorous and distinctive personalities for the great world of the future, it is their portion to die out and disappear.[73]

Quite properly, this unforgiveable passage has often been adduced in a kind of case for the prosecution against Wells as a eugenic racist.[74] The reality is more nuanced, perhaps, but only just: Wells said other, better things, but he said this too.

As the closing section of the novel shows, succumbing to the beast flesh is not only a threat out there in the colonies and the tropics. London is full of Beast Men. Anxieties about degeneration were a characteristic of the *fin de siècle*, given articulation in a variety of different discourses, from the quasi-sociological jeremiad of Max Nordau's influential

[71] Josiah Clark Nott and George R. Gliddon, *Types of Mankind: or, Ethnological Researches* (Philadelphia, 1854).

[72] Darwin, *Descent of Man*, 205.

[73] Wells, *Anticipations, Works*, vol. iv, p. 274.

[74] See, for example, Carey, *The Intellectuals and the Masses*, 125.

Degeneration (1892) to the informed evolutionism of E. Ray Lankester's
Degeneration: A Chapter in Darwinism (1880), written by a distinguished professor of Zoology at University College London (and later
at Oxford), who was a former pupil of Huxley and a future scientific
adviser to Wells himself.[75] As Sally Ledger and Roger Luckhurst write,
degeneration was 'one of the most influential concepts in late-Victorian
culture', and one of its implications was that evolution could flow in
both directions.[76] Degeneration was ripe for exploitation in fiction.[77]
Wells, in fact, had already exploited this anxiety with his portrayal of the
degenerated human beings the Eloi and Morlocks in *The Time Machine*.

   Nordau, in particular, was keen to expose what he saw as the degen-
erate figure in the arts. Oscar Wilde caused Nordau particular anxiety. After a long and hysterical denunciation of Wilde's dress, manner,
and writings, Nordau concludes that 'Oscar Wilde apparently admires
immorality, crime and sin'.[78] Though Nordau does not name Wilde's
homosexuality, this is very evidently at the root of his revulsion.
Oscar Wilde's trial took place in 1895, the same year as the publication of the English translation of *Degeneration*. In complex ways, as
Wells was later to acknowledge in the Atlantic Edition, the shadow of
the Wilde trial looms over *Moreau*:

There was a scandalous trial about that time, the graceless and pitiless down-
fall of a man of genius, and the story was the response of an imaginative mind
to the reminder that humanity is but animal rough-hewn to a reasonable
shape and in perpetual internal conflict between instinct and injunction.[79]

Is it Moreau himself, 'a man of genius' 'howled out of the country' by
public opinion, of whom Wells is thinking here? Or is it Montgomery,
'an outcast from civilisation [. . .] Simply because—eleven years ago,
I lost my head for ten minutes on a foggy night' (p. 18). The London
fog conceals secrets: Wilde wrote approvingly of the beauty of the
fog, in a way that drove Nordau apoplectic: 'so silly as to require no

   [75] Lankester gave Wells scientific advice for *An Englishman Looks at the World* (1914),
and most particularly for the bestselling *Outline of History* (1920).
   [76] Sally Ledger and Roger Luckurst (eds.), *The Fin de Siècle: A Reader in Cultural
History c.1880–1900* (Oxford, 2000), 1.
   [77] For influential studies of degeneration and culture, see Daniel Pick, *Faces of
Degeneration: A European Disorder c. 1848–c.1918* (Cambridge, 1989); William Greenslade,
Degeneration, Culture and the Novel, 1880–1940 (Cambridge, 1994).
   [78] Nordau, *Degeneration* (New York, 1895), 320.
   [79] Wells, 'Preface to Volume II', *Works*, Atlantic Edition, vol. ii, p. ix.

refutation', he concludes after a long and detailed analysis of Wilde's writings on London fogs.[80] *Moreau* constantly hints at a sexual relationship between Montgomery and the Beast Folk, most particularly M'Ling. 'Montgomery . . . interferes in their affairs', Moreau tells Prendick. 'He's ashamed of it, but I believe he half-likes some of these beasts' (p. 69). Nineteenth-century sexual discourse often conflated homosexuality and bestiality. In a laudatory, front-page review of the translation of *Degeneration* in 1895, the *Weekly Sun* wrote:

it is a manly, healthy, and badly-needed protest against some of the inanities, and—the word is not too strong—bestialities which raise their brazen and brutal heads in the literature of our time; and it is entitled, therefore, to the admiration of every honest, pure, and manly man.[81]

As Ed Cohen suggests in commenting on this passage, the unspoken referent here is clearly Oscar Wilde himself, 'since the imputation of "bestialities" to both his writing and his life had been the stuff of newspaper headlines for the three months preceding the review'.[82]

Perhaps characteristically, *The Island of Doctor Moreau* divides against itself here, simultaneously sympathetic towards and horrified by the Wilde trial and its implications. H. G. Wells could be a charitable and sympathetic writer. In 1896, the same year as *Moreau*, he also published *The Wheels of Chance*, the narrative of Mr Hoopdriver, a clerical Everyman who has a series of small adventures while on a bicycling holiday. *The Wheels of Chance* is the precursor of such beloved and fundamentally warm-hearted novels as *Kipps: The Story of a Simple Soul* (1905), or *The History of Mr Polly* (1910). Hoopdriver, Kipps, and Polly are all versions of Wells, or more properly portrayals of one version of Wells, the bright and self-improving draper's assistant from Bromley. But Wells could also be a rebarbative and nihilistic writer, given to viewing the world through the lens of anger, hatred, and disgust. *The Island of Doctor Moreau* obviously falls into this latter category. It is as difficult a novel today as it was for its first readers. It is his fundamental contradiction, the impossibility of classifying him as this kind of writer or that, which makes Wells so enduringly fascinating. We will always be uneasy in the face of his work, and for that reason we should always want to read it.

---

[80] Nordau, *Degeneration*, 322.

[81] Ed Cohen, *Talk on the Wilde Side: Towards a Genealogy of Discourse on Male Sexualities* (London, 1993), 17.   [82] Cohen, *Talk on the Wilde Side*, 17.

NOTE ON THE TEXT

EDITING H. G. Wells has been compared, with some justification, to walking though a minefield.[1] Like many of Wells's works, there are a number of different editions of *The Island of Doctor Moreau*, each one of which has its particular appeal and poses its particular challenges. Some modern editions derive from the 1924 Atlantic Edition of Wells's collected works, which the author himself seems to have thought definitive, but which is often problematic. In the case of *Moreau*, the Atlantic version leaves out the 'Introduction' ascribed to Prendick's nephew, which is crucial not least because it firmly situates the action of the novel in the vicinity of the Galapagos Islands. Furthermore, the Atlantic version was in turn based on the 1913 William Heinemann edition, which introduced a number of typographical errors into the text, which subsequent editors have then silently had to correct. There are good grounds, therefore, for wanting to use the first edition, published in London by William Heinemann in 1896, and this is the edition used here. I have drawn attention to significant textual differences and errors in the Explanatory Notes.

All editors draw on each other's findings, and I have benefited greatly from the work done by previous editors of *The Island of Doctor Moreau*, most particularly by Robert M. Philmus and by Patrick Parrinder.[2] Philmus's 'Variorum Text' contains a definitive account (if anything can be definitive in the world of Wells textual scholarship) of the genesis of *Moreau* across its manuscripts and different editions.

The manuscript versions of *The Island of Doctor Moreau* can be found in the H. G. Wells Papers, 1845–1946, Rare Book and Manuscript Library, University of Illinois at Urbana-Champaign, MS 01/01/MSS00071 File ID 001/C14.04.06.

---

[1] Patrick Parrinder, 'Disagreeing Over *The Definitive Time Machine*, Again', *Science Fiction Studies* 17 (March 1990), 121.

[2] H. G. Wells, *The Island of Doctor Moreau: A Variorum Text*, ed. Robert M. Philmus (Athens, Ga.: University of Georgia Press, 1993); H. G. Wells, *The Island of Doctor Moreau*, ed. Patrick Parrinder, introd. Margaret Atwood and notes by Steven McLean (London: Penguin, 2005).

SELECT BIBLIOGRAPHY

Life and Letters

Sherborne, Michael, *H. G. Wells: Another Kind of Life* (London, 2010). The best modern biography of HGW.

Wells, H. G., *The Correspondence of H. G. Wells*, 4 vols., ed. David C. Smith (London, 1998).

—— *Experiment in Autobiography: Discoveries and Conclusions of a Very Ordinary Brain (Since 1866)* (New York, 1934).

Critical Studies

Carey, John, *The Intellectuals and the Masses: Pride and Prejudice among the Literary Intelligentsia, 1880–1939* (London, 1992).

Daly, Nicholas, *Modernism, Romance and the Fin de Siècle: Popular Fiction and British Culture, 1880–1914* (Cambridge, 1999).

Ferguson, Christine, *Language, Science and Popular Fiction in the Victorian Fin-de-Siècle* (London, 2006).

Hendershot, Cyndy, *The Animal Within: Masculinity and the Gothic* (Ann Arbor, 1998).

Hurley, Kelly, *The Gothic Body: Sexuality, Materialism and Degeneration at the Fin de Siècle* (Cambridge, 1996).

James, Simon J., *Maps of Utopia: H. G. Wells, Modernity, and the End of Culture* (Oxford, 2012).

Keating, Peter, *The Haunted Study: A Social History of the English Novel 1875–1914* (London, 1989).

Killeen, Jarlath, *Gothic Literature 1825–1914* (Cardiff, 2009).

McLean, Steven, *The Early Fiction of H. G. Wells: Fantasies of Science* (London, 2009).

Parrinder, Patrick (ed.), *H. G. Wells: The Critical Heritage* (London, 1972).

Partington, John S., *Building Cosmopolis: The Political Thought of H. G. Wells* (London, 2003).

Trotter, David, *The English Novel in History, 1895–1920* (London, 1993).

Science, Medicine and Beast-Men

Bowler, Peter J., *Evolution: The History of an Idea* (25th anniversary edn., Berkeley and Los Angeles, 2009).

Darwin, Charles, *The Descent of Man*, ed. and introd. James Moore and Adrian Desmond (London, 2004).

French, Richard D., *Antivivisection and Medical Science in Victorian Society* (Princeton, 1975).

Gould, Stephen Jay, *The Mismeasure of Man* (London, 1984).

Huxley, T. H., 'Evolution and Ethics', in *Collected Essays*, ix. *Evolution & Ethics and Other Essays* (London, 1906).

Newton, Michael, *Savage Girls and Wild Boys: A History of Feral Children* (London, 2002).

Otis, Laura (ed.), *Literature and Science in the Nineteenth Century: An Anthology* (Oxford, 2002).

Wells, H. G., *Early Writings in Science and Science Fiction*, ed. Robert Philmus and David Y. Hughes (Berkeley and Los Angeles, 1973).

A CHRONOLOGY OF H. G. WELLS

1866 (21 September) Herbert George Wells born in Bromley, Kent.

1869 Jules Verne, *Twenty Thousand Leagues Under the Sea*; Matthew Arnold, *Culture and Anarchy*.

1870 Elementary Education Act, providing compulsory education for all children 5–13 years old.

1871 Charles Darwin, *The Descent of Man*; Edward Bulwer-Lytton, *The Coming Race*. The Paris Commune: revolutionary period, ending in destruction and massacre.

1872 Samuel Butler, *Erewhon*.

1874–80 HGW pupil at Morley's Academy, Bromley.

1877 Injury to father leaves Wells family in sudden poverty.

1880 HGW apprenticed to Rodgers and Benyer, Drapers, for a month's trial after which he is dismissed; his mother takes position as resident housekeeper, Uppark. Ray Lankester's lecture *Degeneration: A Chapter in Darwinism* a big influence on HGW's biological thought.

1881 Attends Alfred Williams School, then Midhurst Grammar School; apprenticed to Hyde's Drapery Emporium in Southsea.

1882 Robert Louis Stevenson's *Treasure Island*.

1883 HGW's indentures cancelled.

1884 Wins scholarship to Normal School of Science in South Kensington, where T. H. Huxley is dean.

1885 Robert Louis Stevenson, *Strange Case of Dr Jekyll and Mr Hyde*; Richard Jefferies, *After London*.

1886 HGW matriculates. Attends socialist meetings at home of William Morris. Founds and edits *Science School Journal*. Charles Howard Hinton, *Scientific Romances*. Colonial and Indian Exhibition held opposite Normal School of Science.

1887 HGW's first published work in *Science Schools Journal*. Fails geology exam at Normal School, so loses scholarship; teaches at Holt Academy in Wales. Severely injured in accident during football match, resulting in lung haemorrhage which forces him to convalesce. Edward Bellamy, *Looking Backwards*, influential utopian fiction; Gaspar Enrique, *The Time Ship*, Spanish novel featuring time machine. (13 November) 'Bloody Sunday' riots in London, following police charge on marchers in Trafalgar Square.

1888 HGW returns to London; teaches at Henley House School. Publishes three parts of 'The Chronic Argonauts' in _Science Schools Journal_, which is the unfinished first version of _The Time Machine_.

1889 Mark Twain's time travel satire _A Connecticut Yankee in King Arthur's Court_; Elizabeth Corbett, _New Amazonia_, feminist utopia. London Dock Strike.

1890 HGW passes Bachelor of Science exams and is awarded University of London degree. Elected Fellow of the Zoological Society. William Morris, _News from Nowhere_, socialist utopia written as riposte to Bellamy. William Booth, _In Darkest England and the Way Out_.

1891 Tutor for University Tutorial College; publishes essay 'The Rediscovery of the Unique' in _Fortnightly Review_, his first major publication. Marries cousin Isabel Wells. Wilde, _The Picture of Dorian Gray_.

1892 Max Nordau, _Degeneration_.

1893 Recurrence of lung haemorrhage. Publishes _A Text Book of Biology_, his first book. Career as professional journalist begins. T. H. Huxley, _Evolution and Ethics_; Robert Blatchford's political vision _Merrie England_, hugely influential in popularizing socialist ideas; George Griffith's novel about futuristic war in London, _Angel of the Revolution_. Gilbert and Sullivan's satirical _Utopia, Limited_ operetta opens.

1894 HGW elopes with Amy Catherine Robbins ('Jane'). Seven episodes of 'The Time Machine' published by W. E. Henley in _National Observer_. Writes as journalist for _Pall Mall Gazette_, and for the _Saturday Review_ under Frank Harris's editorship. Publishes 'Popularising Science' in _Nature_. Camille Flammarion, _Omega: The Last Days of the World_.

1895 (January–May) _The Time Machine_ serialized in _New Review_, again edited by Henley; HGW declared 'a man of genius' by leading journalist W. T. Stead. Meets G. B. Shaw on opening night of Henry James's play, _Guy Domville_. (May) _The Time Machine_ issued. Also publishes _Select Conversations with an Uncle_; _The Wonderful Visit_; _The Stolen Bacillus_. (April–May) Arrest and prosecution of Oscar Wilde. Decadent movement in retreat. Max Nordau's _Degeneration_; Grant Allen's _The British Barbarians: A Hill-Top Novel_.

1896 _The Island of Doctor Moreau_; _The Wheels of Chance_. Meets novelist George Gissing.

1897 _The Invisible Man_; _The Plattner Story_; _Thirty Strange Stories_; _The Star_; _Certain Personal Matters_. Begins friendship with Arnold Bennett. Queen Victoria's Diamond Jubilee.

1898 *The War of the Worlds.* Suffers from lung damage again; recovering on south coast, meets Henry James and Joseph Conrad. Also travels to Italy, where stays with Gissing. Dislikes Rome intensely.

1899 *When the Sleeper Wakes; Tales of Space and Time.*

1900 House designed and built for HGW at Sandgate in Kent where he becomes near neighbour of Henry James. *Love and Mr Lewisham.*

1901 *Anticipations,* HGW's speculations on the year 2000. Rediscovers Mendel's theory of 'genetics'. *First Men in the Moon,* the last of his early scientific romances. Birth of first son.

1902 Lecture 'The Discovery of the Future' at Royal Institution.

1903 Joins Fabian Society. Birth of second son.

1904 *The Food of the Gods.*

1905 *Kipps; A Modern Utopia.* Einstein's Special Theory of Relativity.

1906 *In the Days of the Comet; The Future in America.* Affairs with Dorothy Richardson, Rosamund Bland, Amber Reeves.

1908 *First and Last Things; The War in the Air; New Worlds for Old.* Resigns from the Fabian Society after dispute with G. B. Shaw.

1909 *Tono-Bungay; Ann Veronica,* HGW's transparently autobiographical account of relationship with Amber Reeves, who gives birth to their daughter Anna-Jane at the end of the year. E. M. Forster publishes 'The Machine Stops', an anti-Wellsian dystopia.

1910 *The History of Mr Polly.* Affair with Elizabeth von Arnim.

1911 *The New Machiavelli.*

1912 *Marriage.* Essay 'The Contemporary Novel' for *Atlantic Monthly.*

1914 Birth of son Anthony, from affair with Rebecca West. Publishes *The World Set Free,* which predicts the invention of the atomic bomb (and became the inspiration for the physicist Leo Szilard). Henry James criticizes HGW in essay 'The Younger Generation'. Great War begins after assassination of Archduke Franz Ferdinand.

1915 *Boon* contains HGW's savage parody of Henry James, which ends their friendship.

1916 Visits western front; publishes *Mr Britling Sees It Through* and *What Is Coming?*

1917 HGW has brief Christian phase. Writes positive review for Joyce's *A Portrait of the Artist as a Young Man.* Russian Revolution.

1918 Joins Ministry of Information. Vote given to women over 30.

1919 Joins committee to set up League of Nations and contributes to *The Idea of a League of Nations;* advocates world government. Publishes his controversial but bestselling *Outline of History.*

1920 Visits Russia and meets Lenin, Trotsky, and Maxim Gorky.

1921 Affair with Margaret Sanger. Red Army victory in Russian Civil War.

1922 *A Short History of the World*. Mussolini in power in Italy.

1923 *Men Like Gods* and *The Dream*. Affair with Odette Keun. Virginia Woolf's essay 'Mr Bennett and Mrs Brown' famously attacks the novels of Bennett and Wells.

1924 The Atlantic Edition of his works published: substantially reworks *The Time Machine*. Zamyatin's Russian dystopia *We*, much influenced by Wells.

1926 Fritz Lang science fiction film *Metropolis*.

1928 *The Open Conspiracy*. Equal voting rights for men and women.

1929 HGW begins to broadcast on BBC. Wall Street Crash.

1930 *The Science of Life*, co-written with son G. P. Wells and Julian Huxley.

1932 *After Democracy*. Aldous Huxley's dystopia *Brave New World*, with one target: Wells's utopian technocracy.

1933 *The Shape of Things of Come*. Adolf Hitler elected as Chancellor of Germany.

1934 HGW interviews both Stalin and F. D. Roosevelt. Publishes *Experiment in Autobiography*.

1935 Alexander Korda's film of *The Shape of Things to Come*.

1938 Lecture tour of Australia.

1939 *The Holy Terror*. Beginning of Second World War.

1940 HGW stays in London during the Blitz.

1941 Last novel, *You Can't Be Too Careful*.

1942 *Science and the World Mind*.

1945 Last books: *The Mind at the End of Its Tether*; *The Happy Turning*. Allied victory in Europe. (January) liberation of Auschwitz; (April) British and American troops find Bergen-Belsen. (August) atomic bombs dropped on Hiroshima and Nagasaki. Election of Labour Government. HGW demonized as scientific technocrat in C. S. Lewis's novel, *That Hideous Strength*.

1946 (13 August) HGW dies in London.

1967 First publication of *H. G. Wells in Love*, the annex of his autobiography about his sexual relationships.

THE ISLAND OF DOCTOR
MOREAU

CONTENTS

INTRODUCTION*

On February the 1st, 1887, the *Lady Vain* was lost by collision with a derelict when about the latitude 1° s. and longitude 107° w.*

On January the 5th, 1888—that is, eleven months and four days after—my uncle, Edward Prendick, a private gentleman, who certainly went aboard the *Lady Vain* at Callao,* and who had been considered drowned, was picked up in latitude 5° 3′ s. and longitude 101° w.* in a small open boat, of which the name was illegible, but which is supposed to have belonged to the missing schooner *Ipecacuanha*.* He gave such a strange account of himself that he was supposed demented. Subsequently, he alleged that his mind was a blank from the moment of his escape from the *Lady Vain*. His case was discussed among psychologists at the time as a curious instance of the lapse of memory consequent upon physical and mental stress. The following narrative was found among his papers by the undersigned, his nephew and heir, but unaccompanied by any definite request for publication.

The only island known to exist in the region in which my uncle was picked up is Noble's Isle, a small volcanic islet, and uninhabited. It was visited in 1891 by HMS *Scorpion*. A party of sailors then landed, but found nothing living thereon except certain curious white moths, some hogs and rabbits, and some rather peculiar rats. No specimen was secured of these. So that this narrative is without confirmation in its most essential particular. With that understood, there seems no harm in putting this strange story before the public, in accordance, as I believe, with my uncle's intentions. There is at least this much in its behalf: my uncle passed out of human knowledge about latitude 5° s. and longitude 105° w.,* and reappeared in the same part of the ocean after a space of eleven months. In some way he must have lived during the interval. And it seems that a schooner call the *Ipecacuanha*, with a drunken captain, John Davis, did start from Arica* with a puma and certain other animals aboard in January 1887, that the vessel was well known at several ports in the South Pacific, and that it finally disappeared from those seas (with a considerable amount of copra* aboard), sailing to its unknown fate from Banya* in December 1887, a date that tallies entirely with my uncle's story.

Charles Edward Prendick

I

IN THE DINGEY OF THE LADY VAIN

I DO not propose to add anything to what has already been written concerning the loss of the *Lady Vain*. As every one knows, she collided with a derelict when ten days out from Callao. The long-boat with seven of the crew was picked up eighteen days after by HM gun-boat *Myrtle*, and the story of their privations has become almost as well known as the far more terrible *Medusa* case.* I have now, however, to add to the published story of the *Lady Vain* another as horrible, and certainly far stranger. It has hitherto been supposed that the four men who were in the dingey perished, but this is incorrect. I have the best of evidence for this assertion—I am one of the four men.

But, in the first place, I must state that there never were four men in the dingey; the number was three. Constans, who was 'seen by the captain to jump into the gig'* (*Daily News*, March 17, 1887), luckily for us, and unluckily for himself, did not reach us. He came down out of the tangle of ropes under the stays of the smashed bowsprit;* some small rope caught his heel as he let go, and he hung for a moment head downward, and then fell and struck a block or spar floating in the water. We pulled towards him, but he never came up.

I say, luckily for us he did not reach us, and I might almost add luckily for himself, for there were only a small breaker* of water and some soddened ship's biscuits with us—so sudden had been the alarm, so unprepared the ship for any disaster. We thought the people on the launch would be better provisioned (though it seems they were not), and we tried to hail them. They could not have heard us, and the next morning when the drizzle cleared—which was not until past mid-day— we could see nothing of them. We could not stand up to look about us because of the pitching of the boat. The sea ran in great rollers, and we had much ado to keep the boat's head to them. The two other men who had escaped so far with me were a man named Helmar, a passenger like myself, and a seaman whose name I don't know, a short sturdy man with a stammer.

We drifted famishing, and, after our water had come to an end, tormented by an intolerable thirst, for eight days altogether. After the second day the sea subsided slowly to a glassy calm. It is quite impossible for the ordinary reader to imagine those eight days. He has not—luckily for himself—anything in his memory to imagine with. After the first day we said little to one another, and lay in our places in the boat and stared at the horizon, or watched, with eyes that grew larger and more haggard every day, the misery and weakness gaining upon our companions. The sun became pitiless. The water ended on the fourth day, and we were already thinking strange things and saying them with our eyes; but it was, I think, the sixth before Helmar gave voice to the thing we all had in mind.* I remember our voices dry and thin, so that we bent towards one another and spared our words. I stood out against it with all my might, was rather for scuttling the boat and perishing together among the sharks that followed us; but when Helmar said that if his proposal was accepted we should have drink, the sailor came round to him.

I would not draw lots, however, and in the night the sailor whispered to Helmar again and again, and I sat in the bows with my clasp-knife in my hand—though I doubt if I had the stuff in me to fight. And in the morning I agreed to Helmar's proposal, and we handed halfpence* to find the odd man.

The lot fell upon the sailor, but he was the strongest of us and would not abide by it, and attacked Helmar with his hands. They grappled together and almost stood up. I crawled along the boat to them, intending to help Helmar by grasping the sailor's leg, but the sailor stumbled with the swaying of the boat, and the two fell upon the gunwale and rolled overboard together. They sank like stones. I remember laughing at that and wondering why I laughed. The laugh caught me suddenly like a thing from without.

I lay across one of the thwarts* for I know not how long, thinking that if I had the strength I would drink sea-water and madden myself to die quickly. And even as I lay there, I saw, with no more interest than if it had been a picture, a sail comeup towards me over the sky-line. My mind must have been wandering, and yet I remember all that happened quite distinctly. I remember how my head swayed with the seas, and the horizon with the sail above it danced up and down. But I also remember as distinctly that I had a persuasion that I was dead, and that I thought what a jest it was they should come too late by such a little to catch me in my body.

For an endless period, as it seemed to me, I lay with my head on the thwart watching the dancing schooner—she was a little ship, schooner-rigged fore and aft—come up out of the sea. She kept tacking to and fro in a widening compass, for she was sailing dead into the wind. It never entered my head to attempt to attract attention, and I do not remember anything distinctly after the sight of her side, until I found myself in a little cabin aft. There's a dim half-memory of being lifted up to the gangway and of a big red countenance, covered with freckles and surrounded with red hair, staring at me over the bulwarks. I also had a disconnected impression of a dark face with extraordinary eyes close to mine, but that I thought was a night-mare, until I met it again. I fancy I recollect some stuff being poured in between my teeth. And that is all.

II

THE MAN WHO WAS GOING NOWHERE

THE cabin in which I found myself was small, and rather untidy. A youngish man with flaxen hair, a bristly straw-coloured moustache, and a dropping nether lip was sitting and holding my wrist. For a minute we stared at one another without speaking. He had watery grey eyes, oddly void of expression.

Then just overhead came a sound like an iron bedstead being knocked about and the low angry growling of some large animal. At the same time the man spoke again.

He repeated his question: 'How do you feel now?'

I think I said I felt all right. I could not recollect how I had got there. He must have seen the question in my face, for my voice was inaccessible to me.

'You were picked up in a boat—starving. The name on the boat was the *Lady Vain*, and there were spots of blood on the gunwale.'* At the same time my eye caught my hand, so thin that it looked like a dirty skin purse full of loose bones, and all the business of the boat came back to me.

'Have some of this,' said he, and gave me a dose of some scarlet stuff, iced.

It tasted like blood, and made me feel stronger.

'You were in luck,' said he, 'to get picked up by a ship with a medical man aboard.' He spoke with a slobbering articulation, with the ghost of a lisp.

'What ship is this?' I said slowly, hoarse from my long silence.

'It's a little trader from Arica and Callao. I never asked where she came from in the beginning. Out of the land of born fools, I guess. I'm a passenger myself from Arica. The silly ass who owns her—he's captain too, named Davis—he's lost his certificate or something. You know the kind of man—calls the thing the *Ipecacuanha*—of all silly infernal names, though when there's much of a sea without any wind she certainly acts according.'*

Then the noise overhead began again, a snarling growl and the voice of a human being together. Then another voice telling some 'Heaven-forsaken idiot' to desist.

'You were nearly dead,' said my interlocutor. 'It was a very near thing indeed. But I've put some stuff into you now. Notice your arms sore? Injections. You've been insensible for nearly thirty hours.'

I thought slowly. I was distracted now by the yelping of a number of dogs. 'Am I eligible for solid food?' I asked.

'Thanks to me,' he said. 'Even now the mutton is boiling.'

'Yes,' I said, with assurance; 'I could eat some mutton.'

'But,' said he, with a momentary hesitation, 'you know I'm dying to hear of how you came to be alone in the boat.' I thought I detected a certain suspicion in his eyes.

'*Damn that howling!*'

He suddenly left the cabin, and I heard him in violent controversy with some one, who seemed to me to talk gibberish in response to him. The matter sounded as though it ended in blows, but in that I thought my ears were mistaken. Then he shouted at the dogs and returned to the cabin.

'Well?' said he, in the doorway. 'You were just beginning to tell me.'

I told him my name, Edward Prendick, and how I had taken to natural history as a relief from the dulness of my comfortable independence. He seemed interested in this. 'I've done some science myself—I did my Biology at University College,*—getting out the ovary of the earthworm and the radula* of the snail and all that. Lord! it's ten years ago. But go on, go on—tell me about the boat.'

He was evidently satisfied with the frankness of my story, which I told in concise sentences enough—for I felt horribly weak,—and when it was finished he reverted at once to the topic of natural history and his own biological studies. He began to question me closely about Tottenham Court Road and Gower Street.* 'Is Caplatzi* still flourishing? What a shop that was!' He had evidently been a very ordinary medical student, and drifted incontinently to the topic of music-halls. He told me some anecdotes. 'Left it all,' he said, 'ten years ago. How jolly it all used to be! But I made a young ass of myself. . . . Played myself out before I was twenty-one. I daresay it's all different now. . . . But I must look up that ass of a cook and see what he's doing to your mutton.'

The growling overhead was renewed, so suddenly and with so much savage anger that it startled me. 'What's that?' I called after him, but the door had closed. He came back again with the boiled mutton, and I was so excited by the appetising smell of it, that I forgot the noise of the beast forthwith.

After a day of alternate sleep and feeding I was so far recovered as to be able to get from my bunk to the scuttle* and see the green seas trying to keep pace with us. I judged the schooner was running before the wind. Montgomery—that was the name of the flaxen-haired man— came in again as I stood there, and I asked him for some clothes. He lent me some duck things* of his own, for those I had worn in the boat, he said, had been thrown overboard. They were rather loose for me, for he was large, and long in his limbs.

He told me casually that the captain was three-parts drunk in his own cabin. As I assumed the clothes I began asking him some questions about the destination of the ship. He said the ship was bound to Hawaii, but that it had to land him first.

'Where?' said I.

'It's an island. . . . Where I live. So far as I know, it hasn't got a name.'

He stared at me with his nether lip dropping, and looked so wilfully stupid of a sudden that it came into my head that he desired to avoid my questions. I had the discretion to ask no more.

III

THE STRANGE FACE

We left the cabin and found a man at the companion* obstructing our way. He was standing on the ladder with his back to us, peering over the combing of the hatchway.* He was, I could see, a mis-shapen man, short, broad, and clumsy, with a crooked back, a hairy neck, and a head sunk between his shoulders. He was dressed in dark blue serge, and had peculiarly thick coarse black hair. I heard the unseen dogs growl furiously, and forthwith he ducked back, coming into contact with the hand I put out to fend him off from myself. He turned with animal swiftness.

In some indefinable way the black face thus flashed upon me shocked me profoundly. It was a singularly deformed one. The facial part projected, forming something dimly suggestive of a muzzle, and the huge half-open mouth showed as big white teeth as I had ever seen in a human mouth. His eyes were bloodshot at the edges, with scarcely a rim of white round the hazel pupils. There was a curious glow of excitement in his face.

'Confound you!' said Montgomery. 'Why the devil don't you get out of the way?' The black-faced man started aside without a word.

I went on up the companion, instinctively staring at him as I did so. Montgomery stayed at the foot for a moment. 'You have no business here, you know,' he said, in a deliberate tone. 'Your place is forward.'

The black-faced man cowered. 'They . . . won't have me forward.' He spoke slowly, with a queer hoarse quality in his voice.

'Won't have you forward!' said Montgomery in a menacing voice. 'But I tell you to go.' He was on the brink of saying something further, then looked up at me suddenly and followed me up the ladder. I had paused halfway through the hatchway, looking back, still astonished beyond measure at the grotesque ugliness of this black-faced creature. I had never beheld such a repulsive and extraordinary face before, and yet—if the contradiction is credible—I experienced at the same time an odd feeling that in some way I *had* already encountered exactly the features and gestures that now amazed me. Afterwards it occurred to me that probably I had seen him as I was lifted aboard, and yet that scarcely satisfied my suspicion of a previous acquaintance. Yet how one could have set eyes on so singular a face and have forgotten the precise occasion passed my imagination.

Montgomery's movement to follow me released my attention, and I turned and looked about me at the flush deck of the little schooner. I was already half prepared by the sounds I had heard for what I saw. Certainly I never beheld a deck so dirty. It was littered with scraps of carrot, shreds of green stuff, and indescribable filth. Fastened by chains to the mainmast were a number of grisly staghounds,* who now began leaping and barking at me, and by the mizzen* a huge puma was cramped in a little iron cage, far too small even to give it turning-room. Further under the starboard bulwark* were some big hutches containing a number of rabbits, and a solitary llama was squeezed in a mere box of a cage forward. The dogs were muzzled by leather straps. The only human being on deck was a gaunt and silent sailor at the wheel.

The patched and dirty spankers* were tense before the wind, and up aloft the little ship seemed carrying every sail she had. The sky was clear, the sun midway down the western sky; long waves, capped by the breeze with froth, were running with us. We went past the steersman to the taffrail* and saw the water come foaming under the stern, and the bubbles go dancing and vanishing in her wake. I turned and surveyed the unsavoury length of the ship.

'Is this an ocean menagerie?' said I.

'Looks like it,' said Montgomery.

'What are these beasts for? Merchandise, curios? Does the captain think he is going to sell them somewhere in the South Seas?'

'It looks like it, doesn't it?' said Montgomery, and turned towards the wake again.

Suddenly we heard a yelp and a volley of furious blasphemy coming from the companion hatchway, and the deformed man with the black face clambered up hurriedly. He was immediately followed by a heavy red-haired man in a white cap. At the sight of the former the stag-hounds, who had all tired of barking at me by this time, became furiously excited, howling and leaping against their chains. The black hesitated before them, and this gave the red-haired man time to come up with him and deliver a tremendous blow between the shoulder-blades. The poor devil went down like a felled ox, and rolled in the dirt among the furiously excited dogs. It was lucky for him they were muzzled. The red-haired man gave a yawp of exultation and stood staggering and, as it seemed to me, in serious danger of either going backwards down the companion hatchway, or forwards upon his victim.

So soon as the second man had appeared, Montgomery had started violently. 'Steady on there!' he cried, in a tone of remonstrance. A couple of sailors appeared on the forecastle.*

The black-faced man, howling in a singular voice, rolled about under the feet of the dogs. No one attempted to help him. The brutes did their best to worry him, butting their muzzles at him. There was a quick dance of their lithe grey bodies over the clumsy prostrate figure. The sailors forward shouted to them as though it was admirable sport. Montgomery gave an angry exclamation, and went striding down the deck. I followed him.

In another second the black-faced man had scrambled up and was staggering forward. He stumbled up against the bulwark by the main shrouds,* where he remained panting and glaring over his shoulder at the dogs. The red-haired man laughed a satisfied laugh.

'Look here, captain,' said Montgomery, with his lisp a little accentuated, gripping the elbows of the red-haired man; 'this won't do.'

I stood behind Montgomery. The captain came half round and regarded him with the dull and solemn eyes of a drunken man. 'Wha' won't do?' he said; and added, after looking sleepily into Montgomery's face for a minute, 'Blasted Sawbones!'

With a sudden movement he shook his arms free, and after two ineffectual attempts stuck his freckled fists into his side-pockets.

'That man's a passenger,' said Montgomery. 'I'd advise you to keep your hands off him.'

'Go to hell!' said the captain loudly. He suddenly turned and staggered towards the side. 'Do what I like on my own ship,' he said.

I think Montgomery might have left him then—seeing the brute was drunk. But he only turned a shade paler, and followed the captain to the bulwarks.

'Look here, captain,' he said. 'That man of mine is not to be ill-treated. He has been hazed* ever since he came aboard.'

For a minute alcoholic fumes kept the captain speechless. 'Blasted Sawbones!' was all he considered necessary.

I could see that Montgomery had one of those slow pertinacious* tempers that will warm day after day to a white heat and never again cool to forgiveness, and I saw too that this quarrel had been some time growing. 'The man's drunk,' said I, perhaps officiously; 'you'll do no good.'

Montgomery gave an ugly twist to his dropping lip. 'He's always drunk. Do you think that excuses his assaulting his passengers?'

'My ship,' began the captain, waving his hand unsteadily towards the cages, 'was a clean ship. Look at it now.' It was certainly anything but clean. 'Crew,' continued the captain, 'clean respectable crew.'

'You agreed to take the beasts.'

'I wish I'd never set eyes on your infernal island. What the devil . . . want beasts for on an island like that? Then that man of yours . . . Understood he was a man. He's a lunatic. And he hadn't no business aft. Do you think the whole damned ship belongs to you?'

'Your sailors began to haze the poor devil as soon as he came aboard.'

'That's just what he is—he's a devil, an ugly devil. My men can't stand him. *I* can't stand him. None of us can't stand him. Nor *you* either.'

Montgomery turned away. '*You* leave that man alone, anyhow,' he said, nodding his head as he spoke.

But the captain meant to quarrel now. He raised his voice: 'If he comes this end of the ship again I'll cut his insides out, I tell you. Cut out his blasted insides! Who are *you* to tell *me* what *I'*m to do. I tell you I'm captain of the ship—Captain and Owner. I'm the law here, I tell you—the law and the prophets.* I bargained to take a man and his attendant to and from Arica and bring back some animals. I never bargained to carry a mad devil and a silly Sawbones, a ——'

Well, never mind what he called Montgomery. I saw the latter take a step forward, and interposed. 'He's drunk,' said I. The captain began some abuse even fouler than the last. 'Shut up,' I said, turning on him sharply, for I had seen danger in Montgomery's white face. With that I brought the downpour on myself.

However, I was glad to avert what was uncommonly near a scuffle, even at the price of the captain's drunken ill-will. I do not think I have ever heard quite so much vile language come in a continuous stream from any man's lips before, though I have frequented eccentric company enough. I found some of it hard to endure—though I am a mild-tempered man. But certainly when I told the captain to shut up I had forgotten I was merely a bit of human flotsam, cut off from my resources, and with my fare unpaid, a mere casual dependant on the bounty—or speculative enterprise—of the ship. He reminded me of it with considerable vigour. But at any rate I prevented a fight.

IV

AT THE SCHOONER'S RAIL

THAT night land was sighted after sundown, and the schooner hove to.* Montgomery intimated that was his destination. It was too far to see any details; it seemed to me then simply a low-lying patch of dim blue in the uncertain blue-grey sea. An almost vertical streak of smoke went up from it into the sky.

The captain was not on deck when it was sighted. After he had vented his wrath on me he had staggered below, and I understand he went to sleep on the floor of his own cabin. The mate practically assumed the command. He was the gaunt, taciturn individual we had seen at the wheel. Apparently he too was in an evil temper with Montgomery. He took not the slightest notice of either of us. We dined with him in a sulky silence, after a few ineffectual efforts on my part to talk. It struck me, too, that the men regarded my companion and his animals in a singularly unfriendly manner. I found Montgomery very reticent about his purpose with these creatures, and about his destination, and though I was sensible of a growing curiosity I did not press him.

We remained talking on the quarter-deck until the sky was thick with stars. Except for an occasional sound in the yellow-lit forecastle, and a movement of the animals now and then, the night was very still. The puma lay crouched together, watching us with shining eyes, a black heap in the corner of its cage. The dogs seemed to be asleep. Montgomery produced some cigars.

He talked to me of London in a tone of half-painful reminiscence, asking all kinds of questions about changes that had taken place. He spoke like a man who had loved his life there, and had been suddenly and irrevocably cut off from it. I gossiped as well as I could of this and that. All the time the strangeness of him was shaping itself in my mind, and as I talked I peered at his odd pallid face in the dim light of the binnacle lantern* behind me. Then I looked out at the darkling sea, where in the dimness his little island was hidden.

This man, it seemed to me, had come out of Immensity merely to save my life. To-morrow he would drop over the side and vanish again out of my existence. Even had it been under commonplace circumstances it would have made me a trifle thoughtful. But in the first place was the singularity of an educated man living on this unknown little island, and coupled with that, the extraordinary nature of his luggage. I found myself repeating the captain's question: What did he want with the beasts? Why, too, had he pretended they were not his when I had remarked about them at first? Then again, in his personal attendant there was a bizarre quality that had impressed me profoundly. These circumstances threw a haze of mystery round the man. They laid hold of my imagination and hampered my tongue.

Towards midnight our talk of London died away, and we stood side by side leaning over the bulwarks, and staring dreamily over the silent starlit sea, each pursuing his own thoughts. It was the atmosphere for sentiment, and I began upon my gratitude.

'If I may say it,' said I, after a time, 'you have saved my life.'

'Chance,' he answered; 'just chance.'

'I prefer to make my thanks to the accessible agent.'

'Thank no one. You had the need, and I the knowledge, and I injected and fed you much as I might have collected a specimen. I was bored, and wanted something to do. If I'd been jaded that day, or hadn't liked your face, well—; it's a curious question where you would have been now.'

This damped my mood a little. 'At any rate——' I began.

'It's chance, I tell you,' he interrupted, 'as everything is in a man's life. Only the asses won't see it. Why am I here now—an outcast from civilisation—instead of being a happy man, enjoying all the pleasures of London? Simply because—eleven years ago—I lost my head for ten minutes on a foggy night.'

He stopped. 'Yes?' said I.

'That's all.'

We relapsed into silence. Presently he laughed. 'There's something in this starlight that loosens one's tongue. I'm an ass, and yet somehow I would like to tell you.'

'Whatever you tell me, you may rely upon my keeping to myself. . . . If that's it.'

He was on the point of beginning, and then shook his head doubtfully. 'Don't,' said I. 'It is all the same to me. After all, it is better to keep your secret. There's nothing gained but a little relief, if I respect your confidence. If I don't . . . well?'

He grunted undecidedly. I felt I had him at a disadvantage, had caught him in the mood of indiscretion; and, to tell the truth, I was not curious to learn what might have driven a young medical student out of London. I have an imagination. I shrugged my shoulders, and turned away. Over the taffrail leant a silent black figure, watching the stars. It was Montgomery's strange attendant. It looked over its shoulder quickly with my movement, then looked away again.

It may seem a little thing to you, perhaps, but it came like a sudden blow to me. The only light near us was a lantern at the wheel. The creature's face was turned for one brief instant out of the dimness of the stern towards this illumination, and I saw that the eyes that glanced at me shone with a pale green light.

I did not know then that a reddish luminosity, at least, is not uncommon in human eyes. The thing came to me as stark inhumanity. That black figure, with its eyes of fire, struck down through all my adult thoughts and feelings, and for a moment the forgotten horrors of childhood came back to my mind. Then the effect passed as it had come. An uncouth black figure of a man, a figure of no particular import, hung over the taffrail, against the starlight, and I found Montgomery was speaking to me.

'I'm thinking of turning in, then,' said he; 'if you've had enough of this.'

I answered him incongruously. We went below, and he wished me good-night at the door of my cabin.

That night I had some very unpleasant dreams. The waning moon rose late. Its light struck a ghostly faint white beam across my cabin, and made an ominous shape on the planking by my bunk. Then the stag-hounds woke, and began howling and baying, so that I dreamt fitfully, and scarcely slept until the approach of dawn.

V

THE MAN WHO HAD NOWHERE TO GO*

IN the early morning—it was the second morning after my recovery, and I believe the fourth after I was picked up—I awoke through an avenue of tumultuous dreams, dreams of guns and howling mobs, and became sensible of a hoarse shouting above me. I rubbed my eyes, and lay listening to the noise, doubtful for a little while of my whereabouts. Then came a sudden pattering of bare feet, the sound of heavy objects being thrown about, a violent creaking and rattling of chains. I heard the swish of the water as the ship was suddenly brought round, and a foamy yellow-green wave flew across the little round window and left it streaming. I jumped into my clothes and went on deck.

As I came up the ladder I saw against the flushed sky—for the sun was just rising—the broad back and red hair of the captain, and over his shoulder the puma spinning from a tackle rigged on to the mizzen spanker boom.* The poor brute seemed horribly scared, and crouched in the bottom of its little cage. 'Overboard with 'em!' bawled the captain. 'Overboard with 'em! We'll have a clean ship soon of the whole bilin' of 'em.'*

He stood in my way, so that I had perforce to tap his shoulder to come on deck. He came round with a start, and staggered back a few paces to stare at me. It needed no expert eye to tell that the man was still drunk. 'Hullo!' said he stupidly, and then with a light coming into his eyes, 'Why, it's Mister—Mister——?'

'Prendick,' said I.

'Prendick be damned!' said he. 'Shut Up—that's your name. Mister Shut Up.'

It was no good answering the brute. But I certainly did not expect his next move. He held out his hand to the gangway by which Montgomery stood talking to a massive white-haired man in dirty blue flannels, who had apparently just come aboard. 'That way, Mister Blasted Shut Up. That way,' roared the captain.

Montgomery and his companion turned as he spoke.

'What do you mean?' said I.

'That way, Mister Blasted Shut Up—that's what I mean. Overboard,

Mister Shut Up—and sharp. We're clearing the ship out, cleaning the whole blessed ship out. And overboard you go.'

I stared at him dumbfounded.* Then it occurred to me it was exactly the thing I wanted. The lost prospect of a journey as sole passenger with this quarrelsome sot was not one to mourn over. I turned towards Montgomery.

'Can't have you,' said Montgomery's companion concisely.

'You can't have me!' said I, aghast. He had the squarest and most resolute face I ever set eyes upon.

'Look here,' I began, turning to the captain.

'Overboard,' said the captain. 'This ship ain't for beasts and cannibals, and worse than beasts, any more. Overboard you go . . . Mr Shut Up. If they can't have you, you goes adrift. But anyhow you go! With your Friends. I've done with this blessed island for evermore amen! I've had enough of it.'

'But, Montgomery,' I appealed.

He distorted his lower lip, and nodded his head hopelessly at the grey-haired man beside him, to indicate his powerlessness to help me.'

'I'll see to *you* presently,' said the captain.

Then began a curious three-cornered altercation. Alternately I appealed to one and another of the three men, first to the grey-haired man to let me land, and then to the drunken captain to keep me aboard. I even bawled entreaties to the sailors. Montgomery said never a word; only shook his head. 'You're going overboard, I tell you,' was the captain's refrain. . . . 'Law be damned! I'm king here.'

At last, I must confess, my voice suddenly broke in the middle of a vigorous threat. I felt a gust of hysterical petulance, and went aft, and stared dismally at nothing.

Meanwhile the sailors progressed rapidly with the task of unshipping the packages and caged animals. A large launch with two standing lugs* lay under the lee of the schooner, and into this the strange assortment of goods were swung. I did not then see the hands from the island that were receiving the packages, for the hull of the launch was hidden from me by the side of the schooner.

Neither Montgomery nor his companion took the slightest notice of me, but busied themselves in assisting and directing the four or five sailors who were unloading the goods. The captain went forward, interfering rather than assisting. I was alternately despairful and desperate. Once or twice, as I stood waiting there for things to accomplish themselves, I could not resist an impulse to laugh at my miserable quandary. I felt all the wretcheder for the lack of a breakfast. Hunger and a lack of blood-corpuscles take all the manhood from a man. I perceived pretty clearly that I had not the stamina either to resist what the captain chose to do to expel me, or to force myself upon Montgomery and his companion. So I waited passively upon fate, and the work of transferring Montgomery's possessions to the launch went on as if I did not exist.

Presently that work was finished, and then came a struggle; I was hauled, resisting weakly enough, to the gangway. Even then I noticed the oddness of the brown faces of the men who were with Montgomery in the launch. But the launch was now fully laden, and was shoved off hastily. A broadening gap of green water appeared under me, and I pushed back with all my strength to avoid falling headlong.

The hands in the launch shouted derisively, and I heard Montgomery curse at them. And then the captain, the mate and one of the seamen helping him, ran me aft towards the stern. The dingey of the *Lady Vain* had been towing behind; it was half full of water, had no oars, and was quite unvictualled. I refused to go aboard her, and flung myself full-length on the deck. In the end they swung me into her by a rope—for they had no stern ladder,—and then they cut me adrift.

I drifted slowly from the schooner. In a kind of stupor I watched all hands take to the rigging, and slowly but surely she came round to the wind. The sails fluttered, and then bellied out as the wind came into them. I stared at her weather-beaten side heeling* steeply towards me. And then she passed out of my range of view.

I did not turn my head to follow her. At first I could scarcely believe what had happened. I crouched in the bottom of the dingey, stunned, and staring blankly at the vacant oily sea. Then I realised that I was in that little hell of mine again, now half-swamped. Looking back over the gunwale I saw the schooner standing away from me, with the red-haired captain mocking at me over the taffrail; and, turning towards the island, saw the launch growing smaller as she approached the beach.

Abruptly the cruelty of this desertion became clear to me. I had no means of reaching the land unless I should chance to drift there. I was still weak, you must remember, from my exposure in the boat;

I was empty and very faint, or I should have had more heart. But as it was I suddenly began to sob and weep as I had never done since I was a little child. The tears ran down my face. In a passion of despair I struck with my fists at the water in the bottom of the boat, and kicked savagely at the gunwale. I prayed aloud for God that he would let me die.

VI

THE EVIL-LOOKING BOATMEN

BUT the islanders, seeing I was really adrift, took pity on me. I drifted very slowly to the eastward, approaching the island slantingly, and presently I saw with hysterical relief the launch come round and return towards me. She was heavily laden, and as she drew near I could make out Montgomery's white-haired broad-shouldered companion sitting cramped up with the dogs and several packing-cases in the stern sheets. This individual stared fixedly at me without moving or speaking. The black-faced cripple was glaring at me as fixedly in the bows near the puma. There were three other men besides, strange brutish-looking fellows, at whom the staghounds were snarling savagely. Montgomery, who was steering, brought the boat by me, and, rising, caught and fastened my painter* to the tiller to tow me—for there was no room aboard.

I had recovered from my hysterical phase by this time, and answered his hail as he approached bravely enough. I told him the dingey was nearly swamped, and he reached me a piggin.* I was jerked back as the rope tightened between the boats. For some time I was busy baling.

It was not until I had got the water under—for the water in the dingey had been shipped, the boat was perfectly sound—that I had leisure to look at the people in the launch again.

The white-haired man, I found, was still regarding me steadfastly, but with an expression, as I now fancied, of some perplexity. When my eyes met his he looked down at the staghound that sat between his knees. He was a powerfully built man, as I have said, with a fine forehead and rather heavy features; but his eyes had that odd drooping of the skin above the lids that often comes with advancing years, and the fall of his heavy mouth at the corners gave him an expression of pugnacious resolution. He talked to Montgomery in a tone too low for me to hear. From him my eyes travelled to his three men, and a strange crew they were. I saw only their faces, yet there was something in their faces—I knew not what—that gave me a queer spasm of disgust. I looked steadily at them, and the impression did not pass, though I failed to see what had occasioned it. They seemed to me then to be brown men, but their limbs were oddly swathed in some thin dirty white stuff down even to the fingers and feet. I have never seen men so wrapped up before, and women so only in the East. They wore turbans too, and thereunder peered out their elfin faces at me, faces with protruding lower jaws and bright eyes. They had lank black hair, almost like horse-hair, and seemed, as they sat, to exceed in stature any race of men I have seen. The white-haired man, who I knew was a good six feet in height, sat a head below any one of the three. I found afterwards that really none were taller than myself, but their bodies were abnormally long, and the thigh-part of the leg short and curiously twisted. At any rate they were an amazingly ugly gang, and over the heads of them, under the forward lug, peered the black face of the man whose eyes were luminous in the dark.

As I stared at them they met my gaze, and then first one and then another turned away from my direct stare and looked at me in an odd furtive manner. It occurred to me that I was perhaps annoying them, and I turned my attention to the island we were approaching.

It was low, and covered with thick vegetation, chiefly a kind of palm that was new to me. From one point a thin white thread of vapour rose slantingly to an immense height, and then frayed out like a down feather. We were now within the embrace of a broad bay flanked on either hand by a low promontory. The beach was of dull grey sand, and sloped steeply up to a ridge, perhaps sixty or seventy feet above the sea-level, and irregularly set with trees and undergrowth. Half-way up was a square piebald stone enclosure that I found subsequently was built partly of coral and partly of pumiceous lava.* Two thatched roofs peeped from within this enclosure.

A man stood awaiting us at the water's edge. I fancied, while we were still far off, that I saw some other and very grotesque-looking creatures scuttle into the bushes upon the slope, but I saw nothing of these as we drew nearer. This man was of a moderate size, and with a black negroid face. He had a large, almost lipless mouth, extraordinary lank arms, long thin feet and bow legs, and stood with his heavy face thrust forward staring at us. He was dressed like Montgomery and his white-haired companion, in jacket and trousers of blue serge.

As we came still nearer, this individual began to run to and fro on the beach, making the most grotesque movements. At a word of command from Montgomery the four men in the launch sprang up with singular awkward gestures and struck the lugs. Montgomery steered us round and into a narrow little dock excavated in the beach. Then the man on the beach hastened towards us. This dock, as I call it, was really a mere ditch just long enough at this phase of the tide to take the long-boat.

I heard the bows ground in the sand, staved the dingey off the rudder of the big boat with my piggin, and, freeing the painter, landed. The three muffled men, with the clumsiest movements, scrambled out upon the sand, and forthwith set to landing the cargo, assisted by the man on the beach. I was struck especially with the curious movements of the legs of the three swathed and bandaged boatmen—not stiff they were, but distorted in some odd way, almost as if they were jointed in the wrong place. The dogs were still snarling, and strained at their chains after these men, as the white-haired man landed with them.

The three big fellows spoke to one another in odd guttural tones, and the man, who had waited for us on the beach, began chattering to them excitedly—a foreign language, as I fancied—as they laid hands on some bales piled near the stern. Somewhere I had heard such a voice before, and I could not think where. The white-haired man stood holding in a tumult of six dogs, and bawling orders over their din. Montgomery, having unshipped the rudder, landed likewise, and all set to work at unloading. I was too faint, what with my long fast and the sun beating down on my bare head, to offer any assistance.

Presently the white-haired man seemed to recollect my presence, and came up to me. 'You look,' said he, 'as though you had scarcely breakfasted.'

His little eyes were a brilliant black under his heavy brows. 'I must apologise for that. Now you are our guest, we must make you comfortable—though you are uninvited, you know.'

He looked keenly into my face. 'Montgomery says you are an educated man, Mr Prendick—says you know something of science. May I ask what that signifies?'

I told him I had spent some years at the Royal College of Science, and had done some research in biology under Huxley.* He raised his eyebrows slightly at that.

'That alters the case a little, Mr Prendick,' he said, with a trifle more respect in his manner. 'As it happens, we are biologists here. This is a biological station—of a sort.' His eye rested on the men in white, who were busily hauling the puma, on rollers, towards the walled yard. 'I and Montgomery, at least,' he added.

Then, 'When you will be able to get away, I can't say. We're off the track to anywhere. We see a ship once in a twelvemonth or so.'

He left me abruptly and went up the beach past this group, and, I think, entered the enclosure. The other two men were with Montgomery erecting a pile of smaller packages on a low wheeled truck. The llama was still on the launch with the rabbit-hutches; the staghounds still lashed to the thwarts. The pile of things completed, all three men laid hold of the truck, and began shoving the ton-weight or so upon it after the puma. Presently Montgomery left them, and coming back to me, held out his hand.

'I'm glad,' said he, 'for my own part. That captain was a silly ass. He'd have made things lively for you.'

'It was you,' said I, 'that saved me again.'

'That depends. You'll find this island an infernally rum place, I promise you. I'd watch my goings carefully, if I were you. *He*—' He hesitated, and seemed to alter his mind about what was on his lips. 'I wish you'd help me with these rabbits,' he said.

His procedure with the rabbits was singular. I waded in with him and helped him lug one of the hutches ashore. No sooner was that done than he opened the door of it, and tilting the thing on one end, turned its living contents out on the ground. They fell in a struggling heap one on the top of the other. He clapped his hands, and forthwith they went off with that hopping run of theirs, fifteen or twenty of them, I should think, up the beach. 'Increase and multiply, my friends,' said Montgomery. 'Replenish the island. Hitherto we've had a certain lack of meat here.'

As I watched them disappearing, the white-haired man returned with a brandy flask and some biscuits. 'Something to go on with, Prendick,' said he, in a far more familiar tone than before.

I made no ado, but set to work on the biscuits at once, while the white-haired man helped Montgomery to release about a score more of the rabbits. Three big hutches, however, went up to the house with the puma. The brandy I did not touch, for I have been an abstainer from my birth.

VII

THE reader will perhaps understand that at first everything was so strange about me, and my position was the outcome of such unexpected adventures, that I had no discernment of the relative strangeness of this or that thing about me. I followed the llama up the beach, and was overtaken by Montgomery, who asked me not to enter the stone enclosure. I noticed then that the puma in its cage and the pile of packages, had been placed outside the entrance to this quadrangle.

I turned and saw that the launch had now been unloaded, run out again, and was being beached, and the white-haired man was walking towards us. He addressed Montgomery.

'And now comes the problem of this uninvited guest. What are we to do with him?'

'He knows something of science,' said Montgomery.

'I'm itching to get to work again—with this new stuff,' said the grey-haired man, nodding towards the enclosure. His eyes grew brighter.

'I daresay you are,' said Montgomery, in anything but a cordial tone.

'We can't send him over there, and we can't spare the time to build him a new shanty. And we certainly can't take him into our confidence just yet.'

'I'm in your hands,' said I. I had no idea of what he meant by 'over there.'

'I've been thinking of the same things,' Montgomery answered. 'There's my room with the outer door——'

'That's it,' said the elder man promptly, looking at Montgomery, and all three of us went towards the enclosure. 'I'm sorry to make a mystery, Mr Prendick—but you'll remember you're uninvited. Our little establishment here contains a secret or so, is a kind of Bluebeard's Chamber,* in fact. Nothing very dreadful really—to a sane man. But just now—as we don't know you——'

'Decidedly,' said I; 'I should be a fool to take offence at any want of confidence.'

He twisted his heavy mouth into a faint smile—he was one of those saturnine people who smile with the corners of the mouth down,—and bowed his acknowledgment of my complaisance. The main entrance to the enclosure we passed; it was a heavy wooden gate, framed in iron and locked, with the cargo of the launch piled outside it; and at the corner we came to a small doorway I had not previously observed. The grey-haired man produced a bundle of keys from the pocket of his greasy blue jacket, opened this door, and entered. His keys and the elaborate locking up of the place, even while it was still under his eye, struck me as peculiar.

I followed him, and found myself in a small apartment, plainly but not uncomfortably furnished, and with its inner door, which was slightly ajar, opening into a paved courtyard. This inner door Montgomery at once closed. A hammock was slung across the darker corner of the room, and a small unglazed window, defended by an iron bar, looked out towards the sea.

This, the grey-haired man told me, was to be my apartment, and the inner door, which, 'for fear of accidents,' he said, he would lock on the other side, was my limit inward. He called my attention to a convenient deck-chair before the window, and to an array of old books, chiefly, I found, surgical works and editions of the Latin and Greek classics—languages I cannot read wi h any comfort*—on a shelf near the hammock. He left the room by the outer door, as if to avoid opening the inner one again.

'We usually have our meals in here,' said Montgomery, and then, as if in doubt, went out after the other. 'Moreau,' I heard him call, and for the moment I do not think I noticed. Then as I handled the books on the shelf it came up in consciousness: where had I heard the name of Moreau before?

I sat down before the window, took out the biscuits that still remained to me, and ate them with an excellent appetite. 'Moreau?'

Through the window I saw one of those unaccountable men in white lugging a packing-case along the beach. Presently the window-frame hid him. Then I heard a key inserted and turned in the lock behind me. After a little while I heard, through the locked door, the noise of the staghounds, which had now been brought up from the beach. They were not barking, but sniffing and growling in a curious fashion. I could hear the rapid patter of their feet, and Montgomery's voice soothing them.

I was very much impressed by the elaborate secrecy of these two men regarding the contents of the place, and for some time I was thinking of that, and of the unaccountable familiarity of the name of Moreau. But so odd is the human memory, that I could not then recall that well-known name in its proper connection. From that my thoughts went to the indefinable queerness of the deformed and white-swathed man on the beach. I never saw such a gait, such odd motions, as he pulled at the box. I recalled that none of these men had spoken to me, though most of them I had found looking at me at one time or another in a peculiar furtive manner, quite unlike the frank stare of your unsophisticated savage. I wondered what language they spoke. They had all seemed remarkably taciturn, and when they did speak, endowed with very uncanny voices. What was wrong with them? Then I recalled the eyes of Montgomery's ungainly attendant.

Just as I was thinking of him, he came in. He was now dressed in white, and carried a little tray with some coffee and boiled vegetables thereon. I could hardly repress a shuddering recoil as he came, bending amiably, and placed the tray before me on the table.

Then astonishment paralysed me. Under his stringy black locks I saw his ear! It jumped upon me suddenly, close to my face. The man had pointed ears, covered with a fine brown fur!

'Your breakfast, sair,' he said. I stared at his face without attempting to answer him. He turned and went towards the door, regarding me oddly over his shoulder.

I followed him out with my eyes, and as I did so, by some odd trick of unconscious cerebration, there came surging into my head the phrase: 'The Moreau—Hollows' was it? 'The Moreau——?' Ah! It sent my memory back ten years. 'The Moreau Horrors.' The phrase drifted loose in my mind for a moment, and then I saw it in red lettering on a little buff-coloured pamphlet, that to read made one shiver and creep. Then I remembered distinctly all about it. That long-forgotten pamphlet came back with startling vividness to my mind. I had been a mere lad then, and Moreau was, I suppose, about fifty; a prominent and masterful physiologist, well known in scientific circles for his extraordinary imagination and his brutal directness in discussion. Was this the same Moreau? He had published some very astonishing facts in connection with the transfusion of blood,* and, in addition, was known to be doing valuable work on morbid growths. Then suddenly his career was closed. He had to leave England. A journalist obtained access to his laboratory in the capacity of laboratory assistant, with the deliberate intention of making sensational exposures;

and by the help of a shocking accident—if it was an accident—his gruesome pamphlet became notorious. On the day of its publication, a wretched dog, flayed and otherwise mutilated, escaped from Moreau's house.

It was in the silly season,* and a prominent editor, a cousin of the temporary laboratory assistant, appealed to the conscience of the nation. It was not the first time that conscience has turned against the methods of research. The doctor was simply howled out of the country. It may be he deserved to be, but I still think the tepid support of his fellow-investigators and his desertion by the great body of scientific workers, was a shameful thing. Yet some of his experiments, by the journalist's account, were wantonly cruel. He might perhaps have purchased his social peace by abandoning his investigations, but he apparently preferred the latter, as most men would who have once fallen under the overmastering spell of research. He was unmarried, and had indeed nothing but his own interests to consider. . . .

I felt convinced that this must be the same man. Everything pointed to it. It dawned upon me to what end the puma and the other animals, which had now been brought with other luggage into the enclosure behind the house, were destined; and a curious faint odour, the halitus* of something familiar, an odour that had been in the background of my consciousness hitherto, suddenly came forward into the forefront of my thoughts. It was the antiseptic odour of the operating-room. I heard the puma growling through the wall, and one of the dogs yelped as though it had been struck.

Yet surely, and especially to another scientific man, there was nothing so horrible in vivisection* as to account for this secrecy. And by some odd leap in my thoughts the pointed ears and luminous eyes of Montgomery's attendant came back again before me with the sharpest definition. I stared before me out at the green sea, frothing under a freshening breeze, and let these and other strange memories of the last few days chase each other through my mind.

What could it mean? A locked enclosure on a lonely island, a notorious vivisector, and these crippled and distorted men? . . .

VIII

MONTGOMERY interrupted my tangle of mystification and suspicion about one, and his grotesque attendant followed him with a tray bearing bread, some herbs, and other eatables, a flask of whisky, a jug of water, and three glasses and knives. I glanced askance at this strange creature, and found him watching me with his queer, restless eyes. Montgomery said he would lunch with me, but that Moreau was too pre-occupied with some work to come.

'Moreau!' said I; 'I know that name.'

'The devil you do!' said he. 'What an ass I was to mention it to you. I might have thought. Anyhow, it will give you an inkling of our—mysteries. Whisky?'

'No thanks—I'm an abstainer.'

'I wish I'd been. But it's no use locking the door after the steed is stolen. It was that infernal stuff led to my coming here. That and a foggy night. I thought myself in luck at the time when Moreau offered to get me off. It's queer. . . .'

'Montgomery,' said I, suddenly, as the outer door closed; 'why has your man pointed ears?'

'Damn!' he said, over his first mouthful of food. He stared at me for a moment, and then repeated, 'Pointed ears?'

'Little points to them,' said I, as calmly as possible, with a catch in my breath; 'and a fine black fur at the edges.'

He helped himself to whisky and water with great deliberation. 'I was under the impression . . . that his hair covered his ears.'

'I saw them as he stooped by me to put that coffee you sent to me on the table. And his eyes shine in the dark.'

By this time Montgomery had recovered from the surprise of my question. 'I always thought,' he said deliberately, with a certain accentuation of his flavouring of lisp; 'that there *was* something the matter with his ears. From the way he covered them. . . . What were they like?'

I was persuaded from his manner that this ignorance was a pretence. Still, I could hardly tell the man that I thought him a liar. 'Pointed,' I said; 'rather small and furry—distinctly furry. But the whole man is one of the strangest beings I ever set eyes on.'

A sharp, hoarse cry of animal pain came from the enclosure behind us. Its depth and volume testified to the puma. I saw Montgomery wince.

'Yes?' he said.

'Where did you pick the creature up?'

'Er—San Francisco. . . . He's an ugly brute, I admit. Half-witted, you know. Can't remember where he came from. But I'm used to him, you know. We both are. How does he strike you?'

'He's unnatural,' I said. 'There's something about him. . . . Don't think me fanciful, but it gives me a nasty little sensation, a tightening of my muscles, when he comes near me. It's a touch. . . . of the diabolical, in fact.'

Montgomery had stopped eating while I told him this. 'Rum,' he said. '*I* can't see it.'

He resumed his meal. 'I had no idea of it,' he said, and masticated. 'The crew of the schooner . . . must have felt it the same. . . . Made a dead set at the poor devil. . . . You saw the captain?'

Suddenly the puma howled again, this time more painfully. Montgomery swore under his breath. I had half a mind to attack him about the men on the beach. Then the poor brute within gave vent to a series of short, sharp screams.

'Your men on the beach,' said I; 'what race are they?'

'Excellent fellows, aren't they?' said he absent-mindedly, knitting his brows as the animal yelled out sharply. I said no more. There was another outcry worse than the former. He looked at me with his dull grey eyes, and then took some more whisky. He tried to draw me into a discussion about alcohol, professing to have saved my life with it. He seemed anxious to lay stress on the fact that I owed my life to him. I answered him distractedly. Presently our meal came to an end, the misshapen monster with the pointed ears cleared away, and Montgomery left me alone in the room again. All the time he was in a state of ill-concealed irritation at the noise of the vivisected puma. He spoke of his odd want of nerve, and left me to the obvious application.

I found myself that the cries were singularly irritating, and they grew in depth and intensity as the afternoon wore on. They were painful at first, but their constant resurgence at last altogether upset my balance. I flung aside a crib of Horace* I had been reading, and began to clench my fists, to bite my lips, and pace the room.

Presently I got to stopping my ears with my fingers.

The emotional appeal of those yells grew upon me steadily, grew at last to such an exquisite expression of suffering that I could stand it in that confined room no longer. I stepped out of the door into the slumberous heat of the late afternoon, and walking past the main entrance—locked again I noticed—turned the corner of the wall.

The crying sounded even louder out of doors. It was as if all the pain in the world had found a voice. Yet had I known such pain was in the next room, and had it been dumb, I believe—I have thought since—I could have stood it well enough. It is when suffering finds a voice and sets our nerves quivering that this pity comes troubling us. But in spite of the brilliant sunlight and the green fans of the trees waving in the soothing sea-breeze, the world was a confusion, blurred with drifting black and red phantasms, until I was out of earshot of the house in the chequered wall.

IX

THE THING IN THE FOREST

I STRODE through the undergrowth that clothed the ridge behind the house, scarcely heeding whither I went, passed on through the shadow of a thick cluster of straight-stemmed trees beyond it, and so presently found myself some way on the other side of the ridge, and descending towards a streamlet that ran through a narrow valley. I paused and listened. The distance I had come, or the intervening masses of thicket, deadened any sound that might be coming from the enclosure. The air was still. Then with a rustle a rabbit emerged, and went scampering up the slope before me. I hesitated, and sat down in the edge of the shade.

The place was a pleasant one. The rivulet was hidden by the luxuriant vegetation of the banks, save at one point, where I caught a triangular patch of its glittering water. On the further side I saw through a bluish haze a tangle of trees and creepers, and above these again the luminous blue of the sky. Here and there a splash of white or crimson marked the blooming of some trailing epiphyte.* I let my eyes wander over this scene for a while, and then began to turn over in my mind again the strange peculiarities of Montgomery's man. But it was too hot to think elaborately, and presently I fell into a tranquil state midway between dozing and waking.

From this I was aroused, after I know not how long, by a rustling amidst the greenery on the other side of the stream. For a moment I could see nothing but the waving summits of the ferns and reeds. Then suddenly upon the bank of the stream appeared something—at first I could not distinguish what it was. It bowed its head to the water and began to drink. Then I saw it was a man, going on all-fours like a beast!

He was clothed in bluish cloth, and was of a copper-coloured hue, with black hair. It seemed that grotesque ugliness was an invariable character of these islanders. I could hear the suck of the water at his lips as he drank.

I leant forward to see him better, and a piece of lava, detached by my hand, went pattering down the slope. He looked up guiltily, and his eyes met mine. Forthwith he scrambled to his feet and stood wiping his clumsy hand across his mouth and regarding me. His legs were scarcely half the length of his body. So, staring one another out of countenance, we remained for perhaps the space of a minute. Then, stopping to look back once or twice, he slunk off among the bushes to the right of me, and I heard the swish of the fronds grow faint in the distance and die away. Every now and then he regarded me with a steadfast stare. Long after he had disappeared I remained sitting up staring in the direction of his retreat. My drowsy tranquillity had gone.

I was startled by a noise behind me, and, turning suddenly, saw the flapping white tail of a rabbit vanishing up the slope. I jumped to my feet.

The apparition of this grotesque half-bestial creature had suddenly populated the stillness of the afternoon for me. I looked around me rather nervously, and regretted that I was unarmed. Then I thought that the man I had just seen had been clothed in bluish cloth, had not been naked as a savage would have been, and I tried to persuade myself from that fact that he was after all probably a peaceful character, that the dull ferocity of his countenance belied him.

Yet I was greatly disturbed at the apparition. I walked to the left along the slope, turning my head about and peering this way and that among the straight stems of the trees. Why should a man go on all-fours and drink with his lips? Presently I heard an animal wailing again, and taking it to be the puma, I turned about and walked in a direction diametrically opposite to the sound. This led me down to the stream, across which I stepped and pushed my way up through the undergrowth beyond.

I was startled by a great patch of vivid scarlet on the ground, and going up to it found it to be a peculiar fungus branched and corrugated like a foliaceous lichen, but deliquescing into slime* at the touch. And then in the shadow of some luxuriant ferns I came upon an unpleasant thing, the dead body of a rabbit, covered with shining flies, but still warm, and with the head torn off. I stopped aghast at the sight of the scattered blood. Here at least was one visitor to the island disposed of!

There were no traces of other violence about it. It looked as though it had been suddenly snatched up and killed. And as I stared at the little furry body came the difficulty of how the thing had been done. The vague dread that had been in my mind since I had seen the inhuman face of the man at the stream grew distincter as I stood there.

I began to realise the hardihood of my expedition among these unknown people. The thicket about me became altered to my imagination. Every shadow became something more than a shadow, became an ambush, every rustle became a threat. Invisible things seemed watching me.

I resolved to go back to the enclosure on the beach. I suddenly turned away and thrust myself violently—possibly even frantically—through the bushes, anxious to get a clear space about me again.

I stopped just in time to prevent myself emerging upon an open space. It was a kind of glade in the forest made by a fall; seedlings were already starting up to struggle for the vacant space, and beyond, the dense growth of stems and twining vines and splashes of fungus and flowers closed in again. Before me, squatting together upon the fungoid ruins of a huge fallen tree, and still unaware of my approach, were three grotesque human figures. One was evidently a female. The other two were men. They were naked, save for swathings of scarlet cloth about the middles, and their skins were of a dull pinkish drab colour, such as I had seen in no savages before. They had fat heavy chinless faces, retreating foreheads,* and a scant bristly hair upon their heads. Never before had I seen such bestial-looking creatures.

They were talking, or at least one of the men was talking to the other two, and all three had been too closely interested to heed the rustling of my approach. They swayed their heads and shoulders from side to side. The speaker's words came thick and sloppy, and though I could hear them distinctly I could not distinguish what he said. He seemed to me to be reciting some complicated gibberish. Presently his articulation became shriller, and spreading his hands he rose to his feet.

At that the others began to gibber in unison, also rising to their feet, spreading their hands, and swaying their bodies in rhythm with their chant. I noticed then the abnormal shortness of their legs and their lank clumsy feet. All three began slowly to circle round, raising and stamping their feet and waving their arms; a kind of tune crept into their rhythmic recitation, and a refrain—'Aloola' or 'Baloola' it sounded like. Their eyes began to sparkle and their ugly faces to brighten with an expression of strange pleasure. Saliva dropped from their lipless mouths.

Suddenly, as I watched their grotesque and unaccountable gestures, I perceived clearly for the first time what it was that had offended me, what had given me the two inconsistent and conflicting impressions of utter strangeness and yet of the strangest familiarity. The three creatures engaged in this mysterious rite were human in shape, and yet human beings with the strangest air about them of some familiar animal. Each of these creatures, despite its human form, its rag of clothing, and the rough humanity of its bodily form, had woven into it, into its movements, into the expression of its countenance, into its whole presence, some now irresistible suggestion of a hog, a swinish taint, the unmistakable mark of the beast.*

I stood overcome by this amazing realisation, and then the most horrible questionings came rushing into my mind. They began leaping in the air, first one and then the other, whooping and grunting. Then one slipped, and for a moment was on all-fours, to recover indeed forthwith. But that transitory gleam of the true animalism of these monsters was enough.

I turned as noiselessly as possible, and becoming every now and then rigid with the fear of being discovered as a branch cracked or a leaf rustled, I pushed back into the bushes. It was long before I grew bolder and dared to move freely.

My one idea for the moment was to get away from these foul beings, and I scarcely noticed that I had emerged upon a faint pathway amidst the trees. Then, suddenly traversing a little glade, I saw with an unpleasant start two clumsy legs among the trees, walking with noiseless footsteps parallel with my course, and perhaps thirty yards away from me. The head and upper part of the body were hidden by a tangle of creeper. I stopped abruptly, hoping the creature did not see me. The feet stopped as I did. So nervous was I that I controlled an impulse to headlong flight with the utmost difficulty.

Then, looking hard, I distinguished through the interlacing network the head and body of the brute I had seen drinking. He moved his head. There was an emerald flash in his eyes as he glanced at me from the shadow of the trees, a half-luminous colour, that vanished as he turned his head again. He was motionless for a moment, and then with noiseless tread began running through the green confusion. In another moment he had vanished behind some bushes. I could not see him, but I felt that he had stopped and was watching me again.

What on earth was he—man or animal? What did he want with me? I had no weapon, not even a stick. Flight would be madness. At any rate the Thing, whatever it was, lacked the courage to attack me.

Setting my teeth hard I walked straight towards him. I was anxious not to show the fear that seemed chilling my backbone. I pushed through a tangle of tall white-flowered bushes, and saw him twenty yards beyond, looking over his shoulder at me and hesitating. I advanced a step or two looking steadfastly into his eyes.

'Who are you?' said I. He tried to meet my gaze.

'No!' he said suddenly, and, turning, went bounding away from me through the undergrowth. Then he turned and stared at me again. His eyes shone brightly out of the dusk under the trees.

My heart was in my mouth, but I felt my only chance was bluff, and walked steadily towards him. He turned again and vanished into the dusk. Once more I thought I caught the glint of his eyes, and that was all.

For the first time I realised how the lateness of the hour might affect me. The sun had set some minutes since, the swift dusk of the tropics was already fading out of the eastern sky, and a pioneer moth fluttered silently by my head. Unless I would spend the night among the unknown dangers of the mysterious forest, I must hasten back to the enclosure.

The thought of a return to that pain-haunted refuge was extremely disagreeable, but still more so was the idea of being overtaken in the open by darkness, and all that darkness might conceal. I gave one more look into the blue shadows that had swallowed up this odd creature, and then retraced my way down the slope towards the stream, going as I judged in the direction from which I had come.

I walked eagerly, perplexed by all these things, and presently found myself in a level place among scattered trees. The colourless clearness that comes after the sunset flush was darkling. The blue sky above grew momentarily deeper, and the little stars one by one pierced the attenuated light; the interspaces of the trees, the gaps in the further vegetation, that had been hazy blue in the daylight, grew black and mysterious.

I pushed on. The colour vanished from the world, the tree-tops rose against the luminous blue sky in inky silhouette, and all below that outline melted into one formless blackness. Presently the trees grew thinner, and the shrubby undergrowth more abundant. Then there was a desolate space covered with white sand, and then another expanse of tangled bushes.

I was tormented by a faint rustling upon my right hand. I thought at first it was fancy, for whenever I stopped, there was silence, save for the evening breeze in the tree-tops. Then when I went on again there was an echo to my footsteps.

I moved away from the thickets, keeping to the more open ground, and endeavouring by sudden turns now and then to surprise this thing, if it existed, in the act of creeping upon me. I saw nothing, and nevertheless my sense of another presence grew steadily. I increased my pace, and after some time came to a slight ridge, crossed it and turned sharply, regarding it steadfastly from the further side. It came out black and clear-cut against the darkling sky.

And presently a shapeless lump heaved up momentarily against the skyline and vanished again. I felt assured now that my tawny-faced antagonist was stalking me again. And coupled with that was another unpleasant realisation, that I had lost my way.

For a time I hurried on hopelessly perplexed, pursued by that stealthy approach. Whatever it was, the thing either lacked the courage to attack me, or it was waiting to take me at some disadvantage. I kept studiously to the open. At times I would turn and listen, and presently I half-persuaded myself that my pursuer had abandoned the chase, or was a mere creation of my disordered imagination. Then I heard the sound of the sea. I quickened my footsteps almost into a run, and immediately there was a stumble in my rear.

I turned suddenly and stared at the uncertain trees behind me. One black shadow seemed to leap into another. I listened rigid, and heard nothing but the creep of the blood in my ears. I thought that my nerves were unstrung, and that my imagination was tricking me, and turned resolutely towards the sound of the sea again.

In a minute or so the trees grew thinner, and I emerged upon a bare low headland running out into the sombre water. The night was calm and clear, and the reflection of the growing multitude of the stars shivered in the tranquil heaving of the sea. Some way out, the wash upon an irregular band of reef shone with a pallid light of its own. Westward I saw the zodiacal light mingling with the yellow brilliance of the evening star.* The coast fell away from me to the east, and westward it was hidden by the shoulder of the cape. Then I recalled the fact that Moreau's beach lay to the west.

A twig snapped behind me and there was a rustle. I turned and stood facing the dark trees. I could see nothing—or else I could see too much. Every dark form in the dimness had its ominous quality, its peculiar suggestion of alert watchfulness. So I stood for perhaps a minute, and then, with an eye to the trees still, turned westward to cross the headland. And as I moved, one among the lurking shadows moved to follow me.

My heart beat quickly. Presently the broad sweep of a bay to the westward became visible, and I halted again. The noiseless shadow halted a dozen yards from me. A little point of light shone on the further bend of the curve, and the grey sweep of the sandy beach lay faint under the starlight. Perhaps two miles away was that little point of light. To get to the beach I should have to go through the trees where the shadows lurked, and down a bushy slope.

I could see the thing rather more distinctly now. It was no animal, for it stood erect. At that I opened my mouth to speak, and found a hoarse phlegm choked my voice. I tried again, and shouted, 'Who is there?' There was no answer. I advanced a step. The thing did not move; only gathered itself together. My foot struck a stone.

That gave me an idea. Without taking my eyes off the black form before me I stooped and picked up this lump of rock. But at my motion the thing turned abruptly as a dog might have done, and slunk obliquely into the further darkness. Then I recalled a schoolboy expedient against big dogs, twisted the rock into my handkerchief, and gave this a turn round my wrist. I heard a movement further off among the shadows as if the thing was in retreat. Then suddenly my tense excitement gave way; I broke into a profuse perspiration and fell a-trembling, with my adversary routed and this weapon in my hand.

It was some time before I could summon resolution to go down through the trees and bushes upon the flank of the headland to the beach. At last I did it at a run, and as I emerged from the thicket upon the sand I heard some other body come crashing after me.

At that I completely lost my head with fear, and began running along the sand. Forthwith there came the swift patter of soft feet in pursuit. I gave a wild cry and redoubled my pace. Some dim black things about three or four times the size of rabbits went running or hopping up from the beach towards the bushes as I passed. So long as I live I shall remember the terror of that chase. I ran near the water's edge, and heard every now and then the splash of the feet that gained upon me. Far away, hopelessly far, was the yellow light. All the night about us was black and still. Splash, splash came the pursuing feet nearer and nearer. I felt my breath going, for I was quite out of training; it whooped as I drew it, and I felt a pain like a knife at my side.

I perceived the thing would come up with me long before I reached the enclosure, and, desperate and sobbing for breath, I wheeled round upon it and struck at it as it came up to me—struck with all my strength. The stone came out of the sling of the handkerchief as I did so.

As I turned, the thing, which had been running on all-fours, rose to its feet, and the missile fell fair on its left temple. The skull rang loud and the animal-man blundered into me, thrust me back with its hands, and went staggering past me to fall headlong upon the sand with its face in the water. And there it lay still.

I could not bring myself to approach that black heap. I left it there with the water rippling round it under the still stars, and, giving it a wide berth, pursued my way towards the yellow glow of the house. And presently, with a positive effect of relief, came the pitiful moaning of the puma, the sound that had originally driven me out to explore this mysterious island. At that, though I was faint and horribly fatigued, I gathered together all my strength, and began running again towards the light. It seemed to me a voice was calling me.

THE CRYING OF THE MAN

As I drew near the house I saw that the light shone from the open door of my room; and then I heard, coming from out of the darkness at the side of that orange oblong, the voice of Montgomery shouting 'Prendick.'

I continued running. Presently I heard him again. I replied by a feeble 'Hullo!' and in another moment had staggered up to him.

'Where have you been?' said he, holding me at arm's-length, so that the light from the door fell on my face. 'We have both been so busy that we forgot you until about half an hour ago.'

He led me into the room and sat me down in the deck chair. For a while I was blinded by the light. 'We did not think you would start to explore this island of ours without telling us,' he said. And then, 'I was afraid! But . . . what . . . Hullo!'

For my last remaining strength slipped from me, and my head fell forward on my chest. I think he found a certain satisfaction in giving me brandy. 'For God's sake,' said I, 'fasten that door.'

'You've been meeting some of our curiosities, eh?' said he. He locked the door and turned to me again. He asked me no questions, but gave me some more brandy and water, and pressed me to eat. I was in a state of collapse. He said something vague about his forgetting to warn me, and asked me briefly when I left the house and what I had seen. I answered him as briefly in fragmentary sentences. 'Tell me what it all means,' said I, in a state bordering on hysterics.

'It's nothing so very dreadful,' said he. 'But I think you have had about enough for one day.' The puma suddenly gave a sharp yell of pain. At that he swore under his breath. 'I'm damned,' said he, 'if this place is not as bad as Gower Street—with its cats.'

'Montgomery,' said I, 'what was that thing that came after me. Was it a beast or was it a man?'

'If you don't sleep to-night,' he said, 'you'll be off your head to-morrow.'

I stood up in front of him. 'What was that thing that came after me?' I asked.

He looked me squarely in the eyes and twisted his mouth askew.

His eyes, which had seemed animated a minute before, went dull. 'From your account,' said he, 'I'm thinking it was a bogle.'*

I felt a gust of intense irritation that passed as quickly as it came. I flung myself into the chair again and pressed my hands on my forehead. The puma began again.

Montgomery came round behind me and put his hand on my shoulder. 'Look here, Prendick,' he said; 'I had no business to let you drift out into this silly island of ours. But it's not so bad as you feel, man. Your nerves are worked to rags. Let me give you something that will make you sleep. *That* . . . will keep on for hours yet. You must simply get to sleep, or I won't answer for it.'

I did not reply. I bowed forward and covered my face with my hands. Presently he returned with a small measure containing a dark liquid. This he gave me. I took it unresistingly, and he helped me into the hammock.

When I awoke it was broad day. For a little while I lay flat, staring at the roof above me. The rafters, I observed, were made out of the timbers of a ship. Then I turned my head and saw a meal prepared for me on the table. I perceived that I was hungry, and prepared to clamber out of the hammock, which, very politely, anticipating my intention, twisted round and deposited me upon all-fours on the floor.

I got up and sat down before the food. I had a heavy feeling in my head, and only the vaguest memory at first of the things that had happened overnight. The morning breeze blew very pleasantly through the unglazed window, and that and the food contributed to the sense of animal comfort I experienced. Presently the door behind me, the door inward towards the yard of the enclosure, opened. I turned and saw Montgomery's face. 'All right?' said he. 'I'm frightfully busy.' And he shut the door. Afterwards I discovered that he forgot to re-lock it.

Then I recalled the expression of his face the previous night, and with that the memory of all I had experienced reconstructed itself before me. Even as that fear returned to me came a cry from within. But this time it was not the cry of a puma.

I put down the mouthful that hesitated upon my lips, and listened. Silence, save for the whisper of the morning breeze. I began to think my ears had deceived me.

After a long pause I resumed my meal, but with my ears still vigilant. Presently I heard something else very faint and low. I sat as if frozen in my attitude. Though it was faint and low, it moved me more profoundly than all that I had hitherto heard of the abominations behind the wall. There was no mistake this time in the quality of the dim broken sounds, no doubt at all of their source; for it was groaning, broken by sobs and gasps of anguish. It was no brute this time. It was a human being in torment!

And as I realised this I rose, and in three steps had crossed the room, seized the handle of the door into the yard, and flung it open before me.

'Prendick, man! Stop!' cried Montgomery, intervening. A startled deerhound yelped and snarled. There was blood, I saw, in the sink, brown, and some scarlet, and I smelt the peculiar smell of carbolic acid.* Then through an open doorway beyond, in the dim light of the shadow, I saw something bound painfully upon a framework, scarred, red, and bandaged. And then blotting this out appeared the face of old Moreau, white and terrible.

In a moment he had gripped me by the shoulder with a hand that was smeared red, had twisted me off my feet, and flung me headlong back into my own room. He lifted me as though I was a little child. I fell at full length upon the floor, and the door slammed and shut out the passionate intensity of his face. Then I heard the key turn in the lock, and Montgomery's voice in expostulation.

'Ruin the work of a lifetime!' I heard Moreau say.

'He does not understand,' said Montgomery, and other things that were inaudible.

'I can't spare the time yet,' said Moreau.

The rest I did not hear. I picked myself up and stood trembling, my mind a chaos of the most horrible misgivings. Could it be possible, I thought, that such a thing as the vivisection of men was possible? The question shot like lightning across a tumultuous sky. And suddenly the clouded horror of my mind condensed into a vivid realisation of my danger.

It came before my mind with an unreasonable hope of escape, that the outer door of my room was still open to me. I was convinced now, absolutely assured, that Moreau had been vivisecting a human being. All the time since I had heard his name I had been trying to link in my mind in some way the grotesque animalism of the islanders with his abominations; and now I thought I saw it all. The memory of his works in the transfusion of blood recurred to me. These creatures I had seen were the victims of some hideous experiment!

These sickening scoundrels had merely intended to keep me back, to fool me with their display of confidence, and presently to fall upon me with a fate more horrible than death, with torture, and after torture the most hideous degradation it was possible to conceive—to send me off, a lost soul, a beast, to the rest of their Comus rout.* I looked round for some weapon. Nothing. Then, with an inspiration, I turned over the deck chair, put my foot on the side of it, and tore away the side rail. It happened that a nail came away with the wood, and, projecting, gave a touch of danger to an otherwise petty weapon. I heard a step outside, incontinently flung open the door, and found Montgomery within a yard of it. He meant to lock the outer door.

I raised this nailed stick of mine and cut at his face, but he sprang back. I hesitated a moment, then turned and fled round the corner of the house. 'Prendick, man!' I heard his astonished cry. 'Don't be a silly ass, man!'

Another minute, thought I, and he would have had me locked in, and as ready as a hospital rabbit for my fate. He emerged behind the corner, for I heard him shout, 'Prendick!' Then he began to run after me, shouting things as he ran.

This time, running blindly, I went northeastward, in a direction at right angles to my previous expedition. Once, as I went running headlong up the beach, I glanced over my shoulder and saw his attendant with him. I ran furiously up the slope, over it, then turned eastward along a rocky valley, fringed on either side with jungle. I ran for perhaps a mile altogether, my chest straining, my heart beating in my ears, and then, hearing nothing of Montgomery or his man, and feeling upon the verge of exhaustion, I doubled sharply back towards the beach, as I judged, and lay down in the shelter of a cane brake.

There I remained for a long time, too fearful to move, and indeed too fearful even to plan a course of action. The wild scene about me lay sleeping silently under the sun, and the only sound near me was the thin hum of some small gnats that had discovered me. Presently I became aware of a drowsy breathing sound—the soughing of the sea upon the beach.

After about an hour I heard Montgomery shouting my name far away to the north. That set me thinking of my plan of action. As I interpreted it then, this island was inhabited only by these two vivisectors and their animalised victims. Some of these, no doubt, they could press into their service against me, if need arose. I knew both Moreau and Montgomery carried revolvers; and, save for a feeble bar of deal, spiked with a small nail, the merest mockery of a mace, I was unarmed.

So I lay still where I was until I began to think of food and drink. And at that moment the real hopelessness of my position came home to me. I knew no way of getting anything to eat; I was too ignorant of botany to discover any resort of root or fruit that might lie about me; I had no means of trapping the few rabbits upon the island. It grew blanker the more I turned the prospect over. At last, in the desperation of my position, my mind turned to the animal men I had encountered. I tried to find some hope in what I remembered of them. In turn I recalled each one I had seen, and tried to draw some augury of assistance from my memory.

Then suddenly I heard a staghound bay, and at that realised a new danger. I took little time to think, or they would have caught me then, but, snatching up my nailed stick, rushed headlong from my hidingplace towards the sound of the sea. I remember a growth of thorny plants with spines that stabbed like penknives. I emerged, bleeding, and with torn clothes, upon the lip of a long creek opening northward. I went straight into the waves without a minute's hesitation, wading up the creek, and presently finding myself knee-deep in a little stream. I scrambled out at last on the westward bank, and, with my heart beating loudly in my ears, crept into a tangle of ferns to await the issue. I heard the dog—it was only one—draw nearer, and yelp when it came to the thorns. Then I heard no more, and presently began to think I had escaped.

The minutes passed, the silence lengthened out, and at last, after an hour of security, my courage began to return to me.

By this time I was no longer very terrified or very miserable. For I had, as it were, passed the limit of terror and despair. I felt now that my life was practically lost, and that persuasion made me capable of daring anything. I had even a certain wish to encounter Moreau face to face. And, as I had waded into the water, I remembered that if I were too hard pressed at least one path of escape from torment still lay open to me—they could not very well prevent my drowning myself. I had half a mind to drown myself then, but an odd wish to see the whole adventure out, a queer impersonal spectacular interest in myself, restrained me. I stretched my limbs, sore and painful from the pricks of the spiny plants, and stared around me at the trees; and, so suddenly that it seemed to jump out of the green tracery about it, my eyes lit upon a black face watching me.

I saw that it was the simian creature who had met the launch upon the beach. He was clinging to the oblique stem of a palm-tree. I gripped my stick, and stood up facing him. He began chattering. 'You, you, you,' was all I could distinguish at first. Suddenly he dropped from the tree, and in another moment was holding the fronds apart, and staring curiously at me.

I did not feel the same repugnance towards this creature that I had experienced in my encounters with the other Beast Men. 'You,' he said, 'in the boat.' He was a man, then—at least, as much of a man as Montgomery's attendant—for he could talk.

'Yes,' I said, 'I came in the boat. From the ship.'

'Oh!' he said, and his bright restless eyes travelled over me, to my hands, to the stick I carried, to my feet, to the tattered places in my coat, and the cuts and scratches I had received from the thorns. He seemed puzzled at something. His eyes came back to my hands. He held his own hand out, and counted his digits slowly, 'One, Two, Three, Four, Five—eh?'

I did not grasp his meaning then. Afterwards I was to find that a great proportion of these Beast People had malformed hands, lacking sometimes even three digits. But guessing this was in some way a greeting, I did the same thing by way of reply. He grinned with immense satisfaction. Then his quick roving glance went round again. He made a swift movement, and vanished. The fern fronds he had stood between came swishing together.

I pushed out of the brake after him, and was astonished to find him swinging cheerfully by one lank arm from a rope of creepers that looped down from the foliage overhead. His back was to me.

'Hullo!' said I.

He came down with a twisting jump, and stood facing me. 'I say,' said I, 'where can I get something to eat?'

'Eat!' he said. 'Eat man's food now.' And his eyes went back to the swing of ropes. 'At the huts.'

'But where are the huts?'

'Oh!'

'I'm new, you know.'

At that he swung round, and set off at a quick walk. All his motions were curiously rapid. 'Come along,' said he. I went with him to see the adventure out. I guessed the huts were some rough shelter, where he and some more of these Beast People lived. I might perhaps find them friendly, find some handle in their minds to take hold of. I did not know yet how far they had forgotten the human heritage I ascribed them.

My ape-like companion trotted along by my side, with his hands hanging down and his jaw thrust forward. I wondered what memory he might have in him. 'How long have you been on this island?' said I.

'How long?' he asked. And, after having the question repeated, he held up three fingers. The creature was little better than an idiot. I tried to make out what he meant by that, and it seems I bored him. After another question or two, he suddenly left my side and sprang at some fruit that hung from a tree. He pulled down a handful of prickly husks, and went on eating the contents. I noted this with satisfaction, for here, at least, was a hint for feeding. I tried him with some other questions, but his chattering prompt responses were, as often as not, quite at cross-purposes with my question. Some few were appropriate, others quite parrot-like.

I was so intent upon these peculiarities that I scarcely noticed the path we followed. Presently we came to trees, all charred and brown, and so to a bare place covered with a yellow-white incrustation, across which a drifting smoke, pungent in whiffs to nose and eyes, went drifting. On our right, over a shoulder of bare rock, I saw the level blue of the sea. The path coiled down abruptly into a narrow ravine between two tumbled and knotty masses of blackish scoriæ.* Into this we plunged.

It was extremely dark, this passage, after the blinding sunlight reflected from the sulphurous ground. Its walls grew steep, and approached one another. Blotches of green and crimson drifted across my eyes. My conductor stopped suddenly. 'Home,' said he, and I stood in a floor of a chasm that was at first absolutely dark to me. I heard some strange noises, and thrust the knuckles of my left hand into my eycs. I became aware of a disagreeable odour like that of a monkey's cage ill-cleaned. Beyond, the rock opened again upon a gradual slope of sunlit greenery, and on either hand the light smote down through a narrow channel into the central gloom.

XII

THE SAYERS OF THE LAW

THEN something cold touched my hand. I started violently, and saw close to me a dim pinkish thing, looking more like a flayed child than anything else in the world. The creature had exactly the mild but repulsive features of a sloth, the same low forehead and slow gestures. As the first shock of the change of light passed, I saw about me more distinctly. The little sloth-like creature was standing and staring at me. My conductor had vanished.

The place was a narrow passage between high walls of lava, a crack in its knotted flow, and on either side interwoven heaps of sea-mat, palm fans and reeds leaning against the rock, formed rough and impenetrably dark dens. The winding way up the ravine between these was scarcely three yards wide, and was disfigured by lumps of decaying fruit-pulp and other refuse, which accounted for the disagreeable stench of the place.

The little pink sloth creature was still blinking at me when my Ape Man reappeared at the aperture of the nearest of these dens, and beckoned me in. As he did so a slouching monster wriggled out of one of the places further up this strange street, and stood up in featureless silhouette against the bright green beyond, staring at me. I hesitated—had half a mind to bolt the way I had come—and then, determined to go through with the adventure, gripped my nailed stick about the middle, and crawled into the little evil-smelling lean-to after my conductor.

It was a semicircular space, shaped like the half of a bee-hive, and against the rocky wall that formed the inner side of it was a pile of variegated fruits, cocoa-nuts and others. Some rough vessels of lava and wood stood about the floor, and one on a rough stool. There was no fire. In the darkest corner of the hut sat a shapeless mass of darkness that grunted 'Hey!' as I came in, and my Ape Man stood in the dim light of the doorway and held out a split cocoa-nut to me as I crawled into the other corner and squatted down. I took it and began gnawing it, as serenely as possible, in spite of my tense trepidation, and the nearly intolerable closeness of the den. The little pink sloth creature stood in the aperture of the hut, and something else with a drab face and bright eyes came staring over its shoulder.

'Hey,' came out of the lump of mystery opposite. 'It is a man! It is a man!' gabbled my conductor—'a man, a man, a live man, like me.'

'Shut up!' said the voice from the dark, and grunted. I gnawed my cocoa-nut amid an impressive silence. I peered hard into the blackness, but could distinguish nothing. 'It is a man,' the voice repeated. 'He comes to live with us?' It was a thick voice with something in it, a kind of whistling overtone, that struck me as peculiar, but the English accent was strangely good.

The Ape Man looked at me as though he expected something. I perceived the pause was interrogative. 'He comes to live with you,' I said.

'It is a man. He must learn the Law.'

I began to distinguish now a deeper blackness in the black, a vague outline of a hunched-up figure. Then I noticed the opening of the place was darkened by two more heads. My hand tightened on my stick. The thing in the dark repeated in a louder tone, 'Say the words.' I had missed its last remark. 'Not to go on all-Fours; that is the Law'— it repeated in a kind of sing-song.

I was puzzled. 'Say the words,' said the Ape Man, repeating, and the figures in the doorway echoed this with a threat in the tone of their voices. I realised I had to repeat this idiotic formula. And then began the insanest ceremony. The voice in the dark began intoning a mad litany, line by line, and I and the rest to repeat it. As they did so, they swayed from side to side, and beat their hands upon their knees, and I followed their example. I could have imagined I was already dead and in another world. The dark hut, these grotesque dim figures, just flecked here and there by a glimmer of light, and all of them swaying in unison and chanting:—

'Not to go on all-Fours; *that* is the Law. Are we not Men?'*

'Not to suck up Drink; *that* is the Law. Are we not Men?'

'Not to eat Flesh nor Fish;* *that* is the Law. Are we not Men?'

'Not to claw Bark of Trees; *that* is the Law. Are we not Men?'

'Not to chase other Men; *that* is the Law. Are we not Men?'

And so from the prohibition of these acts of folly, on to the prohibition of what I thought then were the maddest, most impossible, and most indecent things one could well imagine. A kind of rhythmic fervour fell on all of us; we gabbled and swayed faster and faster, repeating this amazing law. Superficially the contagion of these brute men was upon me, but deep down within me laughter and disgust struggled together. We ran through a long list of prohibitions, and then the chant swung round to a new formula:—

'*His* is the House of Pain.

'*His* is the Hand that makes.

'*His* is the Hand that wounds.

'*His* is the Hand that heals.'

And so on for another long series, mostly quite incomprehensible gibberish to me, about *Him*, whoever he might be. I could have fancied it was a dream, but never before have I heard chanting in a dream.

'*His* is the lightning-flash,' we sang. '*His* is the deep salt sea.'

A horrible fancy came into my head that Moreau, after animalising these men, had infected their dwarfed brains with a kind of deification of himself. However, I was too keenly aware of white teeth and strong claws about me to stop my chanting on that account. '*His* are the stars in the sky.'

At last that song ended. I saw the Ape Man's face shining with perspiration, and my eyes being now accustomed to the darkness, I saw more distinctly the figure in the corner from which the voice came. It was the size of a man, but it seemed covered with a dull grey hair almost like a Skye terrier.* What was it? What were they all? Imagine yourself surrounded by all the most horrible cripples and maniacs it is possible to conceive, and you may understand a little of my feelings with these grotesque caricatures of humanity about me.

'He is a five-man, a five-man, a five-man . . . like me,' said the Ape Man.

I held out my hands. The grey creature in the corner leant forward. 'Not to run on all-Fours; that is the Law. Are we not Men?' he said. He put out a strangely distorted talon, and gripped my fingers. The thing was almost like the hoof of a deer produced into claws. I could have yelled with surprise and pain. His face came forward and peered at my nails, came forward into the light of the opening of the hut, and I saw with a quivering disgust that it was like the face of neither man nor beast, but a mere shock of grey hair, with three shadowy overarchings to mark the eyes and mouth.

'He has little nails,' said this grisly creature in his hairy beard. 'It is well.'

He threw my hand down, and instinctively I gripped my stick. 'Eat roots and herbs—it is His will,' said the Ape Man.

'I am the Sayer of the Law,' said the grey figure. 'Here come all that be new, to learn the Law. I sit in the darkness and say the Law.'

'It is even so,' said one of the beasts in the doorway.

'Evil are the punishments of those who break the Law. None escape.'

'None escape,' said the Beast Folk, glancing furtively at each another.

'None, none,' said the Ape Man. 'None escape. See! I did a little thing, a wrong thing, once. I jabbered, jabbered, stopped talking. None could understand. I am burnt, branded in the hand. He is great, he is good!'

'None escape,' said the grey creature in the corner.

'None escape,' said the Beast People, looking askance at one another.

'For every one the want that is bad,' said the grey Sayer of the Law. 'What you will want, we do not know. We shall know. Some want to follow things that move, to watch and slink and wait and spring, to kill and bite, bite deep and rich, sucking the blood. . . . It is bad. "Not to chase other Men; that is the Law. *Are we not Men?* Not to eat Flesh nor Fish; that is the Law. *Are we not Men?*" '

'None escape,' said a dappled brute standing in the doorway.

'For every one the want that is bad,' said the grey Sayer of the Law. 'Some want to go tearing with teeth and hands into the roots of things, snuffing into the earth. . . . It is bad.'

'None escape,' said the men in the door.

'Some go clawing trees, some go scratching at the graves of the dead; some go fighting with foreheads or feet or claws; some bite suddenly, none giving occasion; some love uncleanness.'

'None escape,' said the Ape Man, scratching his calf.

'None escape,' said the little pink sloth creature.

'Punishment is sharp and sure. Therefore learn the Law. Say the words,' and incontinently he began again the strange litany of the Law, and again I and all these creatures began singing and swaying. My head reeled with this jabbering and the close stench of the place, but I kept on, trusting to find presently some chance of a new development. 'Not to go on all-Fours; that is the Law. *Are we not Men?*'

We were making such a noise that I noticed nothing of a tumult outside, until some one, who, I think, was one of the two Swine Men I had seen, thrust his head over the little pink sloth creature and shouted something excitedly, something that I did not catch. Incontinently those at the opening of the hut vanished, my Ape Man rushed out, the thing that had sat in the dark followed him—I only observed it was big and clumsy, and covered with silvery hair,—and I was left alone.

Then before I reached the aperture I heard the yelp of a staghound.

In another moment I was standing outside the hovel, my chair-rail in my hand, every muscle of me quivering. Before me were the clumsy backs of perhaps a score of these Beast People, their misshapen heads half-hidden by their shoulder-blades. They were gesticulating excitedly. Other half-animal faces glared interrogation out of the hovels. Looking in the direction in which they faced I saw coming through the haze under the trees beyond the end of the passage of dens the dark figure and awful white face of Moreau. He was holding the leaping staghound back, and close behind him came Montgomery, revolver in hand.

For a moment I stood horror-struck.

I turned and saw the passages behind me blocked by another heavy brute with a huge grey face and twinkling little eyes, advancing towards me. I looked round and saw to the right of me, and half a dozen yards in front of me, a narrow gap in the wall of rock through which a ray of light slanted into the shadows. 'Stop!' cried Moreau, as I strode towards this, and then, 'Hold him!' At that, first one face turned towards me, and then others. Their bestial minds were happily slow.

I dashed my shoulder into a clumsy monster who was turning to see what Moreau meant, and flung him forward into another. I felt his hands fly round, clutching at me and missing me. The little pink sloth creature dashed at me and I cut it over, gashed down its ugly face with the nail in my stick, and in another minute I was scrambling up a steep side pathway, a kind of sloping chimney out of the ravine. I heard a howl behind me, and cries of 'Catch him!' 'Hold him!' and the grey-faced creature appeared behind me and jammed his huge bulk into the cleft. 'Go on! go on!' they howled. I clambered up the narrow cleft in the rock, and came out upon the sulphur on the westward side of the village of the Beast Men.

That gap was altogether fortunate for me, for the narrow way slanting obliquely upward must have impeded the nearer pursuers. I ran over the white space and down a steep slope through a scattered growth of trees, and came to a low-lying stretch of tall reeds. Through this I pushed into a dark thick undergrowth that was black and succulent under foot. As I plunged into the reeds my foremost pursuers emerged from the gap. I broke my way through this undergrowth for some minutes. The air behind me and about me was soon full of threatening cries. I heard the tumult of my pursuers in the gap up the slope, then the crashing of the reeds, and every now and then the crackling crash of a branch. Some of the creatures roared like excited beasts of prey. The staghound yelped to the left. I heard Moreau and Montgomery shouting in the same direction. I turned sharply to the right. It seemed to me even then that I heard Montgomery shouting for me to run for my life.

Presently the ground gave, rich and oozy, under my feet; but I was desperate, and went headlong into it, struggled through knee-deep, and so came to a winding path among tall canes. The noise of my pursuers passed away to my left. In one place three strange pink hopping animals, about the size of cats, bolted before my footsteps. This pathway ran uphill, across another open space covered with white incrustation, and plunged into a cane brake again.

Then suddenly it turned parallel with the edge of a steep walled gap which came without warning like the haha of an English park*— turned with an unexpected abruptness. I was still running with all my might, and I never saw this drop until I was flying headlong through the air.

I fell on my forearms and head, among thorns, and rose with a torn ear and bleeding face. I had fallen into a precipitous ravine, rocky and thorny, full of a hazy mist that drifted about me in wisps, and with a narrow streamlet, from which this mist came, meandering down the centre. I was astonished at this thin fog in the full blaze of daylight, but I had no time to stand wondering then. I turned to my right, down stream, hoping to come to the sea in that direction, and so have my way open to drown myself. It was only later I found that I had dropped my nailed stick in my fall.

Presently the ravine grew narrower for a space, and carelessly I stepped into the stream. I jumped out again pretty quickly, for the water was almost boiling. I noticed too there was a thin sulphurous scum drifting upon its coiling water. Almost immediately came a turn in the ravine and the indistinct blue horizon. The nearer sea was flashing the sun from a myriad facets. I saw my death before me. But I was hot and panting, with the warm blood oozing out on my face and running pleasantly through my veins. I felt more than a touch of exultation, too, at having distanced my pursuers. It was not in me then to go out and drown myself. I stared back the way I had come.

I listened. Save for the hum of the gnats and the chirp of some small insects that hopped among the thorns, the air was absolutely still. Then came the yelp of a dog, very faint, and a chattering and gibbering, the snap of a whip and voices. They grew louder, then fainter again. The noise receded up the stream and faded away. For a while the chase was over.

But I knew now how much hope of help for me lay in the Beast People.

XIII

A PARLEY

I TURNED again and went on down towards the sea. I found the hot stream broadened out to a shallow weedy sand, in which an abundance of crabs, and long-bodied, many-legged creatures started from my footfall. I walked to the very edge of the salt water, and then I felt I was safe. I turned and stared—arms akimbo—at the thick green behind me, into which the steamy ravine cut like a smoking gash. But as I say, I was too full of excitement, and—a true saying, though those who have never known danger may doubt it—too desperate to die.

Then it came into my head that there was one chance before me yet. While Moreau and Montgomery and their bestial rabble chased me through the island, might I not go round the beach until I came to their enclosure?—make a flank march upon them, in fact, and then with a rock lugged out of their loosely built wall perhaps, smash in the lock of the smaller door and see what I could find—knife, pistol, or what not—to fight them with when they returned? It was at any rate a chance of getting a price for my life.

So I turned to the westward and walked along by the water's edge. The setting sun flashed his blinding heat into my eyes. The slight Pacific tide* was running in with a gentle ripple.

Presently the shore fell away southward and the sun came round upon my right hand. Then suddenly, far in front of me, I saw first one and then several figures emerging from the bushes,—Moreau with his grey staghound, then Montgomery, and two others. At that I stopped.

They saw me and began gesticulating and advancing. I stood watching them approach. The two Beast Men came running forward to cut me off from the undergrowth inland. Montgomery came running also, but straight towards me. Moreau followed slower with the dog.

At last I roused myself from inaction, and turning seaward walked straight into the water. The water was very shallow at first. I was thirty yards out before the waves reached to my waist. Dimly I could see the inter-tidal creatures darting away from my feet.

'What are you doing, man?' cried Montgomery.

I turned, standing waist-deep, and stared at them.

Montgomery stood panting at the margin of the water. His face was bright red with exertion, his long flaxen hair blown about his head, and his dropping nether lip showed his irregular teeth. Moreau was just coming up, his face pale and firm, and the dog at his hand barked at me. Both men had heavy whips. Further up the beach stared the Beast Men.

'What am I doing?—I am going to drown myself,' said I.

Montgomery and Moreau looked at one another. 'Why?' asked Moreau.

'Because that is better than being tortured by you.'

'I told you so,' said Montgomery, and Moreau said something in a low tone.

'What makes you think I shall torture you?' asked Moreau.

'What I saw,' I said. 'And those—yonder.'

'Hush!' said Moreau, and held up his hand.

'I will not,' said I; 'they were men: what are they now? I at least will not be like them.' I looked past my interlocutors. Up the beach were M'ling, Montgomery's attendant, and one of the white swathed brutes from the boat. Further up, in the shadow of the trees, I saw my little Ape Man, and behind him some other dim figures.

'Who are these creatures?' said I, pointing to them, and raising my voice more and more that it might reach them. 'They were men—men like yourselves, whom you have infected with some bestial taint, men whom you have enslaved, and whom you still fear.—You who listen,' I cried, pointing now to Moreau, and shouting past him to the Beast Men, 'You who listen! Do you not see these men still fear you, go in dread of you? Why then do you fear them? You are many——'

'For God's sake,' cried Montgomery, 'stop that, Prendick!'

'Prendick!' cried Moreau.

They both shouted together as if to drown my voice. And behind them lowered the staring faces of the Beast Men, wondering, their deformed hands hanging down, their shoulders hunched up. They seemed, as I fancied then, to be trying to understand me, to remember something of their human past.

I went on shouting, I scarcely remember what. That Moreau and Montgomery could be killed; that they were not to be feared: that was the burthen of what I put into the heads of the Beast People to my own ultimate undoing. I saw the green-eyed man in the dark rags, who had met me on the evening of my arrival, come out from among the trees, and others followed him to hear me better.

At last for want of breath I paused.

'Listen to me for a moment,' said the steady voice of Moreau, 'and then say what you will.'

'Well?' said I.

He coughed, thought, then shouted: 'Latin, Prendick! Bad Latin! Schoolboy Latin! But try and understand. *Hi non sunt homines, sunt animalia qui nos habemus* . . . vivisected.* A humanising process. I will explain. Come ashore.'

I laughed. 'A pretty story,' said I. 'They talk, build houses, cook. They were men. It's likely I'll come ashore.'

'The water just beyond where you stand is deep . . . and full of sharks.'

'That's my way,' said I. 'Short and sharp. Presently.'

'Wait a minute.' He took something out of his pocket that flashed back the sun, and dropped the object at his feet. 'That's a loaded revolver,' said he. 'Montgomery here will do the same. Now we are going up the beach until you are satisfied the distance is safe. Then come and take the revolvers.'

'Not I. You have a third between you.'

'I want you to think over things, Prendick. In the first place, I never asked you to come upon this island. In the next, we had you drugged last night, had we wanted to work you any mischief; and in the next, now your first panic is over, and you can think a little—is Montgomery here quite up to the character you give him? We have chased you for your good. Because this island is full of . . . inimical phenomena. Why should we want to shoot you when you have just offered to drown yourself?'

'Why did you set . . . your people onto me when I was in the hut?'

'We felt sure of catching you and bringing you out of danger. Afterwards we drew away from the scent—for your good.'

I mused. It seemed just possible. Then I remembered something again.

'But I saw,' said I, 'in the enclosure——'

'That was the puma.'

'Look here, Prendick,' said Montgomery. 'You're a silly ass. Come out of the water and take these revolvers, and talk. We can't do anything more then than we could do now.'

I will confess that then, and indeed always, I distrusted and dreaded Moreau. But Montgomery was a man I felt I understood.

'Go up the beach,' said I, after thinking, and added, 'holding your hands up.'

'Can't do that,' said Montgomery, with an explanatory nod over his shoulder. 'Undignified.'

'Go up to the trees, then,' said I, 'as you please.'

'It's a damned silly ceremony,' said Montgomery.

Both turned and faced the six or seven grotesque creatures, who stood there in the sunlight, solid, casting shadows, moving, and yet so incredibly unreal. Montgomery cracked his whip at them, and forthwith they all turned and fled helter-skelter into the trees. And when Montgomery and Moreau were at a distance I judged sufficient, I waded ashore, and picked up and examined the revolvers. To satisfy myself against the subtlest trickery I discharged one at a rounded lump of lava, and had the satisfaction of seeing the stone pulverised and the beach splashed with lead.

Still I hesitated for a moment.

'I'll take the risk,' said I, at last, and with a revolver in each hand I walked up the beach towards them.

'That's better,' said Moreau, without affectation. 'As it is, you have wasted the best part of my day with your confounded imagination.'

And with a touch of contempt that humiliated me he and Montgomery turned and went on in silence before me.

The knot of Beast Men, still wondering, stood back among the trees. I passed them as serenely as possible. One started to follow me, but retreated again when Montgomery cracked his whip. The rest stood silent—watching. They may once have been animals. But I never before saw an animal trying to think.

XIV

DOCTOR MOREAU EXPLAINS

'AND now, Prendick, I will explain,' said Doctor Moreau, so soon as we had eaten and drunk. 'I must confess you are the most dictatorial guest I ever entertained. I warn you that this is the last I do to oblige you. The next thing you threaten to commit suicide about I shan't do—even at some personal inconvenience.'

He sat in my deck chair, a cigar half consumed in his white, dexterous-looking fingers. The light of the swinging lamp fell on his white hair; he stared through the little window out at the starlight. I sat as far away from him as possible, the table between us and the revolvers to hand. Montgomery was not present. I did not care to be with the two of them in such a little room.

'You admit that vivisected human being, as you called it, is, after all, only the puma?' said Moreau. He had made me visit that horror in the inner room to assure myself of its inhumanity.

'It is the puma,' I said, 'still alive, but so cut and mutilated as I pray I may never see living flesh again. Of all vile——'

'Never mind that,' said Moreau. 'At least spare me those youthful horrors. Montgomery used to be just the same. You admit that it is the puma. Now be quiet while I reel off my physiological lecture to you.' And forthwith, beginning in the tone of a man supremely bored, but presently warming a little, he explained his work to me. He was very simple and convincing. Now and then there was a touch of sarcasm in his voice. Presently I found myself hot with shame at our mutual positions.

The creatures I had seen were not men, had never been men. They were animals—humanised animals—triumphs of vivisection.

'You forget all that a skilled vivisector can do with living things,' said Moreau. 'For my own part I'm puzzled why the things I have done here have not been done before. Small efforts of course have been made—amputation, tongue-cutting, excisions. Of course you know a squint may be induced or cured by surgery? Then in the case of excisions you have all kinds of secondary changes, pigmentary disturbances, modifications of the passions, alterations in the secretion of fatty tissue. I have no doubt you have heard of these things?'

'Of course,' said I. 'But these foul creatures of yours——'

'All in good time,' said he, waving his hand at me; 'I am only begin-ning. Those are trivial cases of alteration. Surgery can do better things than that. There is building up as well as breaking down and changing. You have heard, perhaps, of a common surgical operation resorted to in cases where the nose has been destroyed. A flap of skin is cut from the forehead, turned down on the nose, and heals in the new position. This is a kind of grafting in a new position of part of an animal upon itself. Grafting of freshly obtained material from another animal is also possible,—the case of teeth, for example. The grafting of skin and bone is done to facilitate healing. The surgeon places in the middle of the wound pieces of skin snipped from another animal, or fragments of bone from a victim freshly killed. Hunter's cockspur— possibly you have heard of that—flourished on the bull's neck.* And the rhinoceros rats of the Algerian zouaves* are also to be thought of,—monsters manufactured by transferring a slip from the tail of an ordinary rat to its snout, and allowing it to heal in that position.'

'Monsters manufactured!' said I. 'Then you mean to tell me——'

'Yes. These creatures you have seen are animals carven and wrought into new shapes. To that—to the study of the plasticity of living forms— my life has been devoted. I have studied for years, gaining in know-ledge as I go. I see you look horrified, and yet I am telling you nothing new. It all lay in the surface of practical anatomy years ago, but no one had the temerity to touch it. It's not simply the outward form of an animal I can change. The physiology, the chemical rhythm of the creature, may also be made to undergo an enduring modification, of which vaccination and other methods of inoculation with living or dead matter are examples that will, no doubt, be familiar to you. A similar operation is the transfusion of blood, with which subject indeed I began. These are all familiar cases. Less so, and probably far more extensive, were the operations of those mediæval practitioners who made dwarfs and beggar cripples and show-monsters; some vestiges of whose art still remain in the preliminary manipulation of the young mountebank or contortionist. Victor Hugo gives an account of them in *L'Homme qui Rit.** . . . But perhaps my meaning grows plain now. You begin to see that it is a possible thing to transplant tissue from one part of an animal to another, or from one animal to another, to alter its chemical reactions and methods of growth, to modify the articulations of its limbs, and indeed to change it in its most intimate structure?

'And yet this extraordinary branch of knowledge has never been sought as an end, and systematically, by modern investigators, until I took it up! Some such things have been hit upon in the last resort of surgery; most of the kindred evidence that will recur to your mind has been demonstrated, as it were, by accident—by tyrants, by criminals, by the breeders of horses and dogs, by all kinds of untrained clumsy-handed men working for their own immediate ends. I was the first man to take up this question armed with antiseptic surgery, and with a really scientific knowledge of the laws of growth.

'Yet one would imagine it must have been practised in secret before. Such creatures as the Siamese Twins.* . . . And in the vaults of the Inquisition. No doubt their chief aim was artistic torture, but some, at least, of the inquisitors must have had a touch of scientific curiosity. . . .'

'But,' said I. 'These things—these animals *talk*!'

He said that was so, and proceeded to point out that the possibilities of vivisection do not stop at a mere physical metamorphosis. A pig may be educated. The mental structure is even less determinate than the bodily. In our growing science of hypnotism we find the promise of a possibility of replacing old inherent instincts by new suggestions, grafting upon or replacing the inherited fixed ideas. Very much, indeed, of what we call moral education is such an artificial modification and perversion of instinct; pugnacity is trained into cour-ageous self-sacrifice, and suppressed sexuality into religious emotion. And the great difference between man and monkey is in the larynx, he said, in the incapacity to frame delicately different sound-symbols by which thought could be sustained. In this I failed to agree with him, but with a certain incivility he declined to notice my objec-tion. He repeated that the thing was so, and continued his account of his work.

But I asked him why he had taken the human form as a model. There seemed to me then, and there still seems to me now, a strange wickedness in that choice.

He confessed that he had chosen that form by chance. 'I might just as well have worked to form sheep into llamas, and llamas into sheep. I suppose there is something in the human form that appeals to the artistic turn of mind more powerfully than any animal shape can. But I've not confined myself to man-making. Once or twice . . .' He was silent, for a minute perhaps. 'These years! How they have slipped by!

And here I have wasted a day saving your life, and am now wasting an hour explaining myself!'

'But,' said I, 'I still do not understand. Where is your justification for inflicting all this pain? The only thing that could excuse vivisection to me would be some application——'

'Precisely,' said he. 'But you see I am differently constituted. We are on different platforms. You are a materialist.'*

'I am *not* a materialist,' I began hotly.

'In my view—in my view. For it is just this question of pain that parts us. So long as visible or audible pain turns you sick, so long as your own pains drive you, so long as pain underlies your propositions about sin, so long, I tell you, you are an animal, thinking a little less obscurely what an animal feels. This pain——'

I gave an impatient shrug at such sophistry.

'Oh! but it is such a little thing. A mind truly opened to what science has to teach must see that it is a little thing. It may be that, save in this little planet, this speck of cosmic dust, invisible long before the nearest star could be attained—it may be, I say, that nowhere else does this thing called pain occur. But the laws we feel our way towards . . . Why, even on this earth, even among living things, what pain is there?'

He drew a little penknife as he spoke from his pocket, opened the smaller blade and moved his chair so that I could see his thigh. Then, choosing the place deliberately, he drove the blade into his leg and withdrew it.

'No doubt you have seen that before. It does not hurt a pin-prick. But what does it show? The capacity for pain is not needed in the muscle, and it is not placed there; it is but little needed in the skin, and only here and there over the thigh is a spot capable of feeling pain. Pain is simply our intrinsic medical adviser to warn us and stimulate us. All living flesh is not painful, nor is all nerve, not even all sensory nerve. There's no taint of pain, real pain, in the sensations of the optic nerve. If you wound the optic nerve you merely see flashes of light, just as disease of the auditory nerve merely means a humming in our ears. Plants do not feel pain; the lower animals—it's possible that such animals as the starfish and crayfish do not feel pain. Then with men, the more intelligent they become the more intelligently they will see after their own welfare, and the less they will need the goad to keep them out of danger. I never yet heard of a useless thing that was not ground out of existence by evolution sooner or later. Did you? And pain gets needless.

'Then I am a religious man, Prendick, as every sane man must be. It may be I fancy I have seen more of the ways of this world's Maker than you—for I have sought his laws, in *my* way, all my life, while you, I understand, have been collecting butterflies. And I tell you, pleasure and pain have nothing to do with heaven or hell. Pleasure and pain—Bah! What is your theologian's ecstasy but Mahomet's houri* in the dark? This store men and women set on pleasure and pain, Prendick, is the mark of the beast* upon them, the mark of the beast from which they came. Pain! Pain and pleasure—they are for us, only so long as we wriggle in the dust. . . .

'You see, I went on with this research just the way it led me. That is the only way I ever heard of research going. I asked a question, devised some method of getting an answer, and got—a fresh question. Was this possible, or that possible? You cannot imagine what this means to an investigator, what an intellectual passion grows upon him. You cannot imagine the strange colourless delight of these intellectual desires. The thing before you is no longer an animal, a fellow-creature, but a problem. Sympathetic pain—all I know of it I remember as a thing I used to suffer from years ago. I wanted—it was the only thing I wanted—to find out the extreme limit of plasticity in a living shape.'*

'But,' said I, 'the thing is an abomination——'

'To this day I have never troubled about the ethics of the matter. The study of Nature makes a man at last as remorseless as Nature. I have gone on, not heeding anything but the question I was pursuing, and the material has . . . dripped into the huts yonder. . . . It is nearly eleven years since we came here, I and Montgomery and six Kanakas.* I remember the green stillness of the island and the empty ocean about us as though it was yesterday. The place seemed waiting for me.

'The stores were landed and the house was built. The Kanakas founded some huts near the ravine. I went to work here upon what I had brought with me. There were some disagreeable things happened at first. I began with a sheep, and killed it after a day and a half by a slip of the scalpel; I took another sheep and made a thing of pain and fear, and left it bound up to heal. It looked quite human to me when I had finished it; but when I went to it I was discontented with it; it remembered me, and was terrified beyond imagination, and it had no more than the wits of a sheep. The more I looked at it the clumsier it seemed, until at last I put the monster out of its misery. These animals without courage, these fear-haunted pain-driven things, without a spark of pugnacious energy to face torment—they are no good for man-making.

'Then I took a gorilla I had, and upon that, working with infinite care, and mastering difficulty after difficulty, I made my first man. All the week, night and day, I moulded him. With him it was chiefly the brain that needed moulding; much had to be added, much changed. I thought him a fair specimen of the negroid type* when I had done him, and he lay, bandaged, bound, and motionless before me. It was only when his life was assured that I left him, and came into the room again and found Montgomery much as you are. He had heard some of the cries as the thing grew human, cries like those that disturbed *you* so. I didn't take him completely into my confidence at first. And the Kanakas, too, had realised something of it. They were scared out of their wits by the sight of me. I got Montgomery over to me—in a way, but I and he had the hardest job to prevent the Kanakas deserting. Finally they did, and so we lost the yacht. I spent many days educating the brute—altogether I had him for three or four months. I taught him the rudiments of English, gave him ideas of counting, even made the thing read the alphabet. But at that he was slow—though I've met with idiots slower. He began with a clean sheet, mentally; had no memories left in his mind of what he had been. When his scars were quite healed, and he was no longer anything but painful and stiff, and able to converse a little, I took him yonder and introduced him to the Kanakas as an interesting stowaway.

'They were horribly afraid of him at first, somehow—which offended me rather, for I was conceited about him,—but his ways seemed so mild, and he was so abject, that after a time they received him and took his education in hand. He was quick to learn, very imitative and adaptive, and built himself a hovel rather better, it seemed to me, than their own shanties. There was one among the boys, a bit of a missionary, and he taught the thing to read, or at least to pick out letters, and gave him some rudimentary ideas of morality, but it seems the beast's habits were not all that is desirable.

'I rested from work for some days, and was in a mind to write an account of the whole affair to wake up English physiology. Then I came upon the creature squatting up in a tree and gibbering at two of the

Kanakas who had been teasing him. I threatened him, told him the inhumanity of such a proceeding, aroused his sense of shame, and came home resolved to do better before I took my work back to England. I have been doing better; but somehow the things drift back again, the stubborn beast flesh* grows, day by day, back again. . . . I mean to do better things still. I mean to conquer that. This puma . . .

'But that's the story. All the Kanaka boys are dead now. One fell overboard of the launch, and one died of a wounded heel that he poisoned in some way with plant-juice. Three went away in the yacht, and I suppose, and hope, were drowned. The other one . . . was killed. Well—I have replaced them. Montgomery went on much as you are disposed to do at first, and then . . .'

'What became of the other one?' said I sharply,—'the other Kanaka who was killed?'

'The fact is, after I had made a number of human creatures I made a thing—' He hesitated.

'Yes?' said I.

'It was killed.'

'I don't understand,' said I; 'do you mean to say . . .'

'It killed the Kanaka—yes. It killed several other things that it caught. We chased it for a couple of days. It only got loose by accident—I never meant it to get away. It wasn't finished. It was purely an experiment. It was a limbless thing with a horrible face that writhed along the ground in a serpentine fashion. It was immensely strong and in infuriating pain, and it travelled in a rollicking way like a porpoise swimming. It lurked in the woods for some days, doing mischief to all it came across, until we hunted it, and then it wriggled into the northern part of the island, and we divided the party to close in upon it. Montgomery insisted upon coming with me. The man had a rifle, and when his body was found one of the barrels was curved into the shape of an S, and very nearly bitten through. . . . Montgomery shot the thing. . . . After that I stuck to the ideal of humanity—except for little things.'

He became silent. I sat in silence watching his face.

'So for twenty years altogether—counting nine years in England— I have been going on, and there is still something in everything I do that defeats me, makes me dissatisfied, challenges me to further effort. Sometimes I rise above my level, sometimes I fall below it, but always I fall short of the things I dream. The human shape I can get now, almost with ease, so that it is lithe and graceful, or thick and strong; but often there is trouble with the hands and claws—painful things that I dare not shape too freely. But it is in the subtle grafting and re-shaping one must needs do to the brain that my trouble lies. The intelligence is often oddly low, with unaccountable blank ends, unexpected gaps. And least satisfactory of all is something that I cannot touch, somewhere—I cannot determine where—in the seat of the emotions. Cravings, instincts, desires that harm humanity, a strange hidden reservoir to burst suddenly and inundate the whole being of the creature with anger, hate, or fear. These creatures of mine seemed strange and uncanny to you soon as you began to observe them, but to me, just after I make them, they seem to be indisputable human beings. It's afterwards as I observe them that the persuasion fades. First one animal trait, then another, creeps to the surface and stares out at me. . . . But I will conquer yet. Each time I dip a living creature into the bath of burning pain, I say, This time I will burn out all the animal, this time I will make a rational creature of my own. After all, what is ten years? Man has been a hundred thousand in the making.'

He thought darkly. 'But I am drawing near the fastness. This puma of mine . . .'

After a silence: 'And they revert. As soon as my hand is taken from them the beast begins to creep back, begins to assert itself again. . . .'

Another long silence.

'Then you take the things you make into those dens?' said I.

'They go. I turn them out when I begin to feel the beast in them, and presently they wander there. They all dread this house and me. There is a kind of travesty of humanity over there. Montgomery knows about it, for he interferes in their affairs. He has trained one or two of them to our service. He's ashamed of it, but I believe he half-likes some of these beasts. It's his business, not mine. They only sicken me with a sense of failure. I take no interest in them. I fancy they follow in the lines the Kanaka missionary marked out, and have a kind of mockery of a rational life—poor beasts! There's something they call the Law. Sing hymns about "all thine." They build themselves their dens, gather fruit and pull herbs—marry even. But I can see through it all, see into their very souls, and see there nothing but the souls of beasts, beasts that perish—anger, and the lusts to live and gratify themselves. . . . Yet they're odd. Complex, like everything else alive. There is a kind of upward striving in them, part vanity, part waste sexual emotion, part waste curiosity. It only mocks me. . . . I have some hope of that puma; I have worked hard at her head and brain. . . .

'And now,' said he, standing up after a long gap of silence, during which we had each pursued our own thoughts; 'what do you think? Are you in fear of me still?'

I looked at him, and saw but a white-faced white-haired man, with calm eyes. Save for his serenity, the touch almost of beauty that resulted from his set tranquillity, and from his magnificent build, he might have passed muster among a hundred other comfortable old gentlemen. Then I shivered. By way of answer to his second question, I handed him a revolver with either hand.

'Keep them,' he said, and snatched at a yawn. He stood up, stared at me for a moment, and smiled. 'You have had two eventful days,' said he. 'I should advise some sleep. I'm glad it's all clear. Good-night.'

He thought me over for a moment, then went out by the inner door. I immediately turned the key in the outer one.

I sat down again, sat for a time in a kind of stagnant mood, so weary, emotionally, mentally, and physically, that I could not think beyond the point at which he had left me. The black window stared at me like an eye. At last with an effort I put out the lamp, and got into the hammock. Very soon I was asleep.

XV

CONCERNING THE BEAST FOLK

I WOKE early. Moreau's explanation stood before my mind, clear and definite, from the moment of my awakening. I got out of the hammock and went to the door to assure myself that the key was turned. Then I tried the window-bar, and found it firmly fixed. That these man-like creatures were in truth only bestial monsters, mere grotesque travesties of men, filled me with a vague uncertainty of their possibilities that was far worse than any definite fear. A tapping came at the door, and I heard the glutinous accents of M'ling speaking. I pocketed one of the revolvers (keeping one hand upon it), and opened to him.

'Good-morning, sair,' he said, bringing in, in addition to the customary herb breakfast, an ill-cooked rabbit. Montgomery followed him. His roving eye caught the position of my arm, and he smiled askew.

The puma was resting to heal that day; but Moreau, who was singularly solitary in his habits, did not join us. I talked with Montgomery to clear my ideas of the way in which the E east Folk lived. In particular, I was urgent to know how these inhuman monsters were kept from falling upon Moreau and Montgomery, and from rending one another.

He explained to me that the comparative safety of Moreau and himself was due to the limited mental scope of these monsters. In spite of their increased intelligence, and the tendency of their animal instincts to re-awaken, they had certain Fixed Ideas implanted by Moreau in their minds, which absolutely bounded their imaginations. They were really hypnotised, had been told certain things were impossible, and certain things were not to be done, and these prohibitions were woven into the texture of their minds beyond any possibility of disobedience or dispute. Certain matters, however, in which old instinct was at war with Moreau's convenience, were in a less stable condition. A series of propositions called the Law—I had already heard them recited—battled in their minds with the deep-seated, ever rebellious cravings of their animal natures. This Law they were ever repeating, I found, and—ever breaking. Both Montgomery and Moreau displayed particular solicitude to keep them ignorant of the taste of blood. They feared the inevitable suggestions of that flavour.

Montgomery told me that the Law, especially among the feline Beast People, became oddly weakened about nightfall; that then the animal was at its strongest; a spirit of adventure sprang up in them at the dusk; they would dare things they never seemed to dream about by day. To that I owed my stalking by the Leopard Man on the night of my arrival. But during these earlier days of my stay they broke the Law only furtively, and after dark; in the daylight there was a general atmosphere of respect for its multifarious prohibitions.

And here perhaps I may give a few general facts about the island and the Beast People. The island, which was of irregular outline, and lay low upon the wide sea, had a total area, I suppose, of seven or eight square miles.[1] It was volcanic in origin, and was now fringed on three sides by coral reefs. Some fumarolles* to the northward, and a hot spring, were the only vestiges of the forces that had long since originated it. Now and then a faint quiver of earthquake would be sensible, and sometimes the ascent of the spire of smoke would be rendered tumultuous by gusts of steam. But that was all. The population of the island, Montgomery informed me, now numbered rather more than sixty of these strange creations of Moreau's art, not counting the smaller monstrosities which lived in the undergrowth and were without human form. Altogether, he had made nearly a hundred and twenty, but many had died; and others, like the writhing Footless Thing of which he had told me, had come by violent ends. In answer to my question, Montgomery said that they actually bore offspring, but that these generally died. There was no evidence of the inheritance of their acquired human characteristics.* When they lived, Moreau took them and stamped the human form upon them. The females were less numerous than the males, and liable to much furtive persecution in spite of the monogamy the Law enjoined.

It would be impossible for me to describe these Beast People in detail—my eye has had no training in details—and unhappily I cannot sketch. Most striking perhaps in their general appearance was the disproportion between the legs of these creatures and the length of their bodies; and yet—so relative is our idea of grace—my eye became habituated to their forms, and at last I even fell in with their persuasion that my own long thighs were ungainly. Another point was the forward carriage of the head, and the clumsy and inhuman curvature

[1] This description corresponds in every respect to Noble's Isle.—C. E. P.

of the spine. Even the Ape Man lacked that inward sinuous curve of the back that makes the human figure so graceful. Most had their shoulders hunched clumsily, and their short forearms hung weakly at their sides. Few of them were conspicuously hairy—at least, until the end of my time upon the island.

The next most obvious deformity was in their faces, almost all of which were prognathous,* malformed about the ears, with large and protuberant noses, very furry or very bristly hair, and often strangely coloured or strangely placed eyes. None could laugh, though the Ape Man had a chattering titter. Beyond these general characters their heads had little in common; each preserved the quality of its particular species: the human mark distorted but did not hide the leopard, the ox, or the sow, or other animal or animals, from which the creature had been moulded. The voices, too, varied exceedingly. The hands were always malformed; and though some surprised me by their unexpected humanity, almost all were deficient in the number of the digits, clumsy about the finger-nails, and lacking any tactile sensibility.

The two most formidable animal-men were my Leopard Man and a creature made of Hyæna and Swine. Larger than these were the three bull creatures who pulled in the boat. Then came the Silvery Hairy Man, who was also the Sayer of the Law, M'ling, and a satyr-like creature of Ape and Goat. There were three Swine Men and a Swine Woman, a Mare-Rhinoceros creature, and several other females whose sources I did not ascertain. There were several Wolf creatures, a Bear-Bull, and a Saint Bernard Dog Man. I have already described the Ape Man, and there was a particularly hateful (and evil-smelling) old woman made of Vixen and Bear, whom I hated from the beginning. She was said to be a passionate votary of the Law. Smaller creatures were certain dappled youths and my little sloth creature. But enough of this catalogue!

At first I had a shivering horror of the brutes, felt all too keenly that they were still brutes, but insensibly I became a little habituated to the idea of them, and, moreover, I was affected by Montgomery's attitude towards them. He had been with them so long that he had come to regard them as almost normal human beings—his London days seemed a glorious impossible past to him. Only once in a year or so did he go to Arica to deal with Moreau's agent, a trader in animals there. He hardly met the finest type of mankind in that seafaring village of Spanish mongrels. The men aboard ship, he told me, seemed at first just as strange to him as the Beast Men seemed to me,—unnaturally long in the leg, flat in the face, prominent in the forehead, suspicious, dangerous, and cold-hearted. In fact, he did not like men. His heart had warmed to me, he thought, because he had saved my life.

I fancied even then that he had a sneaking kindness for some of these metamorphosed brutes, a vicious sympathy with some of their ways, but that he attempted to veil from me at first.

M'ling, the black-faced man, his attendant, the first of the Beast Folk I had encountered, did not live with the others across the island, but in a small kennel at the back of the enclosure. The creature was scarcely so intelligent as the Ape Man, but far more docile, and the most human-looking of all the Beast Folk, and Montgomery had trained it to prepare food, and indeed to discharge all the trivial domestic offices that were required. It was a complex trophy of Moreau's horrible skill, a bear, tainted with dog and ox, and one of the most elaborately made of all his creatures. It treated Montgomery with a strange tenderness and devotion; sometimes he would notice it, pat it, call it half-mocking, half-jocular names, and so make it caper with extraordinary delight; sometimes he would ill-treat it, especially after he had been at the whisky, kicking it, beating it, pelting it with stones or lighted fusees.* But whether he treated it well or ill, it loved nothing so much as to be near him.

I say I became habituated to the Beast People, that a thousand things that had seemed unnatural and repulsive speedily became natural and ordinary to me. I suppose everything in existence takes its colour from the average hue of our surroundings: Montgomery and Moreau were too peculiar and individual to keep my general impressions of humanity well defined. I would see one of the clumsy bovine creatures who worked the launch treading heavily through the undergrowth, and find myself asking, trying hard to recall, how he differed from some really human yokel trudging home from his mechanical labours; or I would meet the Fox-Bear Woman's vulpine shifty face, strangely human in its speculative cunning, and even imagine I had met it before in some city byway.

Yet every now and then the beast would flash out upon me beyond doubt or denial. An ugly-looking man, a hunchbacked human savage to all appearance, squatting in the aperture of one of the dens, would stretch his arms and yawn, showing with startling suddenness scissor-edged incisors and sabre-like canines, keen and brilliant as knives.

Or in some narrow pathway, glancing with a transitory daring into the eyes of some lithe white-swathed female figure, I would suddenly see (with a spasmodic revulsion) that they had slit-like pupils, or, glancing down, note the curving nail with which she held her shapeless wrap about her. It is a curious thing, by the by, for which I am quite unable to account, that these weird creatures—the females I mean—had in the earlier days of my stay an instinctive sense of their own repulsive clumsiness, and displayed, in consequence, a more than human regard for the decencies and decorum of external costume.

XVI

BUT my inexperience as a writer betrays me, and I wander from the thread of my story. After I had breakfasted with Montgomery he took me across the island to see the fumarolle and the source of the hot spring, into whose scalding waters I had blundered on the previous day. Both of us carried whips and loaded revolvers. While going through a leafy jungle on our road thither we heard a rabbit squealing. We stopped and listened, but we heard no more, and presently we went on our way, and the incident dropped out of our minds. Montgomery called my attention to certain little pink animals with long hind-legs, that went leaping through the undergrowth. He told me they were creatures made of the offspring of the Beast People, that Moreau had invented. He had fancied they might serve for meat, but a rabbit-like habit of devouring their young had defeated this intention. I had already encountered some of these creatures, once during my moonlight flight from the Leopard Man, and once during my pursuit by Moreau on the previous day. By chance, one hopping to avoid us leapt into the hole caused by the uprooting of a wind-blown tree. Before it could extricate itself we managed to catch it. It spat like a cat, scratched and kicked vigorously with its hind-legs, and made an attempt to bite, but its teeth were too feeble to inflict more than a painless pinch. It seemed to me rather a pretty little creature, and as Montgomery stated that it never destroyed the turf by burrowing, and was very cleanly in its habits, I should imagine it might prove a convenient substitute for the common rabbit in gentlemen's parks.

We also saw on our way the trunk of a tree barked in long strips and splintered deeply. Montgomery called my attention to this. 'Not to claw Bark of Trees; *that* is the Law,' he said. 'Much some of them care for it!' It was after this, I think, that we met the Satyr and the Ape Man. The Satyr was a gleam of classical memory on the part of Moreau, his face ovine in expression—like the coarser Hebrew type,—his voice a harsh bleat, his nether extremities Satanic.* He was gnawing the husk of a pod-like fruit as he passed us. Both of them saluted Montgomery.

'Hail,' said they, 'to the Other with the whip!'

'There's a third with a whip now,' said Montgomery. 'So you'd better mind!'

'Was he not made?' said the Ape Man. 'He said—he said he was made.'

The Satyr Man looked curiously at me. 'The Third with the whip, he that walks weeping into the sea, has a thin white face.'

'He has a thin long whip,' said Montgomery.

'Yesterday he bled and wept,' said the Satyr. 'You never bleed nor weep. The Master does not bleed nor weep.'

'Ollendorffian beggar!'* said Montgomery. 'You'll bleed and weep if you don't look out.'

'He has five fingers; he is a five-man like me,' said the Ape Man.

'Come along, Prendick,' said Montgomery, taking my arm, and I went on with him.

The Satyr and the Ape Man stood watching us and making other remarks to each other.

'He says nothing,' said the Satyr. 'Men have voices.'

'Yesterday he asked me of things to eat,' said the Ape Man. 'He did not know.' Then they spoke inaudible things, and I heard the Satyr laughing.

It was on our way back that we came upon the dead rabbit. The red body of the wretched little beast was rent to pieces, many of the ribs stripped white, and the backbone indisputably gnawed.

At that Montgomery stopped. 'Good God!' said he, stooping down and picking up some of the crushed vertebræ to examine them more closely. 'Good God!' he repeated, 'what can this mean?'

'Some carnivore of yours has remembered its old habits,' I said, after a pause. 'This back-bone has been bitten through.'

He stood staring, with his face white and his lip pulled askew. 'I don't like this,' he said slowly.

'I saw something of the same kind,' said I, 'the first day I came here.'

'The devil you did! What was it?'

'A rabbit with its head twisted off.'

'The day you came here?'

'The day I came here. In the undergrowth, at the back of the enclosure, when I came out in the evening. The head was completely wrung off.'

He gave a long low whistle.

'And what is more, I have an idea which of your brutes did the thing. It's only a suspicion, you know. Before I came on the rabbit I saw one of your monsters drinking in the stream.'

'Sucking his drink?'

'Yes.'

'Not to suck your Drink; *that* is the Law. Much the brutes care for the Law, eh—when Moreau's not about?'

'It was the brute who chased me.'

'Of course,' said Montgomery; 'it's just the way with carnivores. After a kill they drink. It's the taste of blood, you know.

'What was the brute like?' he asked. 'Would you know him again?' He glanced about us, standing astride over the mess of dead rabbit, his eyes roving among the shadows and screens of greenery, the lurking-places and ambuscades* of the forest, that bounded us in. 'The taste of blood,' he said again.

He took out his revolver, examined the cartridges in it, and replaced it. Then he began to pull at his dropping lip.

'I think I should know the brute again. I stunned him. He ought to have a handsome bruise on the forehead of him.'

'But then we have to *prove* he killed the rabbit,' said Montgomery. 'I wish I'd never brought the things here.'

I should have gone on, but he stayed there thinking over the man-gled rabbit in a puzzle-headed way. As it was, I went to such a distance that the rabbit's remains were hidden.

'Come on!' I said.

Presently he woke up and came towards me. 'You see,' he said, almost in a whisper, 'they are all supposed to have a fixed idea against eating anything that runs on land. If some brute has by any accident tasted blood . . .'

We went on some way in silence. 'I wonder what can have hap-pened,' he said to himself. Then, after a pause, again: 'I did a foolish thing the other day. That servant of mine . . . I showed him how to skin and cook a rabbit. It's odd . . . I saw him licking his hands . . . It never occurred to me.'

Then: 'We must put a stop to this. I must tell Moreau.'

He could think of nothing else on our homeward journey.

Moreau took the matter even more seriously than Montgomery, and I need scarcely say I was infected by their evident consternation. 'We must make an example,' said Moreau. 'I've no doubt in my own mind that the Leopard Man was the sinner. But how can we prove it? I wish, Montgomery, you had kept your taste for meat in hand, and gone without these exciting novelties. We may find ourselves in a mess yet through it.'

'I was a silly ass,' said Montgomery. 'But the thing's done now. And you said I might have them, you know.'

'We must see to the thing at once,' said Moreau. 'I suppose, if anything should turn up, M'ling can take care of himself?'

'I'm not so sure of M'ling,' said Montgomery. 'I think I ought to know him.'

In the afternoon, Moreau, Montgomery, myself, and M'ling went across the island to the huts in the ravine. We three were armed. M'ling carried the little hatchet he used in chopping firewood, and some coils of wire. Moreau had a huge cowherd's horn slung over his shoulder. 'You will see a gathering of the Beast People,' said Montgomery. 'It's a pretty sight.' Moreau said not a word on the way, but his heavy white-fringed face was grimly set.

We crossed the ravine, down which smoked the stream of hot water, and followed the winding pathway through the cane brakes until we reached a wide area covered over with a thick powdery yellow substance, which I believe was sulphur. Above the shoulder of a weedy bank the sea glittered. We came to a kind of shallow natural amphitheatre, and here the four of us halted. Then Moreau sounded the horn and broke the sleeping stillness of the tropical afternoon. He must have had strong lungs. The hooting note rose and rose amidst its echoes to at last an ear-penetrating intensity. 'Ah!' said Moreau, letting the curved instrument fall to his side again.

Immediately there was a crashing through the yellow canes, and a sound of voices from the dense green jungle that marked the morass through which I had run on the previous day. Then at three or four points on the edge of the sulphurous area appeared the grotesque forms of the Beast People, hurrying towards us. I could not help a creeping horror as I perceived first one and then another trot out from the trees or reeds, and come shambling along over the hot dust. But Moreau and Montgomery stood calmly enough, and, perforce, I stuck beside them. First to arrive was the Satyr, strangely unreal, for all that he cast a shadow, and tossed the dust with his hoofs; after him, from the brake, came a monstrous lout, a thing of horse and rhinoceros, chewing a straw as it came; and then appeared the Swine Woman and two

Wolf Women; then the Fox-Bear Witch with her red eyes in her peaked red face, and then others—all hurrying eagerly. As they came forward they began to cringe towards Moreau and chant, quite regardless of one another, fragments of the latter half of the litany of the Law: '*His* is the Hand that wounds, *His* is the Hand that heals,' and so forth.

As soon as they had approached within a distance of perhaps thirty yards they halted, and bowing on knees and elbows, began flinging the white dust upon their heads. Imagine the scene if you can. We three blue-clad men, with our misshapen black-faced attendant, standing in a wide expanse of sunlit yellow dust under the blazing blue sky, and surrounded by this circle of crouching and gesticulating monstrosities, some almost human, save in their subtle expression and gestures, some like cripples, some so strangely distorted as to resemble nothing but the denizens of our wildest dreams. And beyond, the reedy lines of a cane brake in one direction, a dense tangle of palm-trees on the other, separating us from the ravine with the huts, and to the north the hazy horizon of the Pacific Ocean.

'Sixty-two, sixty-three,' counted Moreau. 'There are four more.'

'I do not see the Leopard Man,' said I.

Presently Moreau sounded the great horn again, and at the sound of it all the Beast People writhed and grovelled in the dust. Then, slinking out of the cane brake, stooping near the ground, and trying to join the dust-throwing circle behind Moreau's back, came the Leopard Man. And I saw that his forehead was bruised. The last of the Beast People to arrive was the little Ape Man. The earlier animals, hot and weary with their grovelling, shot vicious glances at him.

'Cease,' said Moreau, in his firm loud voice, and the Beast People sat back upon their hams and rested from their worshipping.

'Where is the Sayer of the Law?' said Moreau, and the hairy grey monster bowed his face in the dust.

'Say the words,' said Moreau, and forthwith all in the kneeling assembly, swaying from side to side and dashing up the sulphur with their hands, first the right hand and a puff of dust, and then the left, began once more to chant their strange litany.

When they reached 'Not to eat Flesh or Fish; that is the Law,' Moreau held up his lank white hand. '*Stop!*' he cried, and there fell absolute silence upon them all.

I think they all knew and dreaded what was coming. I looked round at their strange faces. When I saw their wincing attitudes and the furtive dread in their bright eyes, I wondered that I had ever believed them to be men.

'That Law has been broken,' said Moreau.

'None escape,' from the faceless creature with the Silvery Hair. 'None escape,' repeated the kneeling circle of Beast People.

'Who is he?' cried Moreau, and looked round at their faces, cracking his whip. I fancied the Hyæna-Swine looked dejected, so too did the Leopard Man. Moreau stopped, facing this creature, who cringed towards him with the memory and dread of infinite torment. 'Who is he?' repeated Moreau, in a voice of thunder.

'Evil is he who breaks the Law,' chanted the Sayer of the Law.

Moreau looked into the eyes of the Leopard Man, and seemed to be dragging the very soul out of the creature.

'Who breaks the Law—' said Moreau, taking his eyes off his victim and turning towards us. It seemed to me there was a touch of exultation in his voice.

'—goes back to the House of Pain,' they all clamoured;—'goes back to the House of Pain, O Master!'

'Back to the House of Pain—back to the House of Pain,' gabbled the Ape Man, as though the idea was sweet to him.

'Do you hear?' said Moreau, turning back to the criminal, 'my frien . . . Hullo!'

For the Leopard Man, released from Moreau's eye, had risen straight from his knees, and now, with eyes aflame and his huge feline tusks flashing out from under his curling lips, leapt towards his tormentor. I am convinced that only the madness of unendurable fear could have prompted this attack. The whole circle of threescore monsters seemed to rise about us. I drew my revolver. The two figures collided. I saw Moreau reeling back from the Leopard Man's blow. There was a furious yelling and howling all about us. Every one was moving rapidly. For a moment I thought it was a general revolt.

The furious face of the Leopard Man flashed by mine, with M'ling close in pursuit. I saw the yellow eyes of the Hyæna-Swine blazing with excitement, his attitude as if he were half-resolved to attack me. The Satyr, too, glared at me over the Hyæna-Swine's hunched shoulders. I heard the crack of Moreau's pistol, and saw the pink flash dart across the tumult. The whole crowd seemed to swing round in the direction of the glint of fire, and I, too, was swung round by the magnetism of the movement. In another second I was running, one of a tumultuous shouting crowd, in pursuit of the escaping Leopard Man.

That is all that I can tell definitely. I saw the Leopard Man strike Moreau, and then everything spun about me, until I was running headlong.

M'ling was ahead, close in pursuit of the fugitive. Behind, their tongues already lolling out, ran the Wolf-Women in great leaping strides. The Swine-Folk followed, squealing with excitement, and the two Bull Men in their swathings of white. Then came Moreau in a cluster of the Beast People, his wide-brimmed straw hat blown off, his revolver in hand, and his lank white hair streaming out. The Hyæna-Swine ran beside me, keeping pace with me, and glancing furtively at me out of his feline eyes, and the others came pattering and shouting behind us.

The Leopard Man went bursting his way through the long canes, which sprang back as he passed and rattled in M'ling's face. We others in the rear found a trampled path for us when we reached the brake. The chase lay through the brake for perhaps a quarter of a mile, and then plunged into a dense thicket, that retarded our movements exceedingly, though we went through it in a crowd together—fronds flicking into our faces, ropy creepers catching us under the chin, or gripping our ankles, thorny plants hooking into and tearing cloth and flesh together.

'He has gone on all-fours through this,' panted Moreau, now just ahead of me.

'None escape,' said the Wolf-Bear, laughing into my face with the exultation of hunting.

We burst out again among rocks, and saw the quarry ahead, running lightly on all-fours, and snarling at us over his shoulder. At that the Wolf-Folk howled with delight. The thing was still clothed, and, at a distance, its face still seemed human, but the carriage of its four limbs was feline, and the furtive droop of its shoulder was distinctly that of a hunted animal. It leapt over some thorny yellow-flowering bushes and was hidden. M'ling was half-way across the space.

Most of us now had lost the first speed of the chase, and had fallen into a longer and steadier stride. I saw, as we traversed the open, that the pursuit was now spreading from a column into a line. The Hyæna-Swine still ran close to me, watching me as it ran, every now and then puckering its muzzle with a snarling laugh.

At the edge of the rocks, the Leopard Man, realising he was making for the projecting cape upon which he had stalked me on the night of my arrival, had doubled in the undergrowth. But Montgomery had seen the manoeuvre, and turned him again.

So, panting, tumbling against rocks, torn by brambles, impeded by ferns and reeds, I helped to pursue the Leopard Man, who had broken the Law, and the Hyæna-Swine ran, laughing savagely, by my side. I staggered on, my head reeling, and my heart beating against my ribs, tired almost to death, and yet not daring to lose sight of the chase, lest I should be left alone with this horrible companion. I staggered on in spite of infinite fatigue and the dense heat of the tropical afternoon.

At last the fury of the hunt slackened. We had pinned the wretched brute into a corner of the island. Moreau, whip in hand, marshalled us all into an irregular line, and we advanced, now slowly, shouting to one another as we advanced, and tightening the cordon about our victim. He lurked, noiseless and invisible, in the bushes through which I had run from him during that midnight pursuit.

'Steady!' cried Moreau; 'steady!' as the ends of the line crept round the tangle of undergrowth, and hemmed the brute in.

''Ware a rush!' came the voice of Montgomery from beyond the thicket.

I was on the slope above the bushes. Montgomery and Moreau beat along the beach beneath. Slowly we pushed in among the fretted network of branches and leaves. The quarry was silent.

'Back to the House of Pain, the House of Pain, the House of Pain!' yelped the voice of the Ape Man, some twenty yards to the right.

When I heard that I forgave the poor wretch all the fear he had inspired in me.

I heard the twigs snap and the boughs swish aside before the heavy tread of the Horse-Rhinoceros upon my right. Then suddenly, through a polygon of green, in the half-darkness under the luxuriant growth, I saw the creature we were hunting. I halted. He was crouched together into the smallest possible compass, his luminous green eyes turned over his shoulder regarding me.

It may seem a strange contradiction in me—I cannot explain the fact,—but now, seeing the creature there in a perfectly animal attitude, with the light gleaming in its eyes, and its imperfectly human face distorted with terror, I realised again the fact of its humanity. In another moment others of its pursuers* would see it, and it would be overpowered and captured, to experience once more the horrible tortures of the enclosure. Abruptly I slipped out my revolver, aimed between its terror-struck eyes, and fired.

As I did so the Hyæna-Swine saw the thing, and flung itself upon it with an eager cry, thrusting thirsty teeth into its neck. All about me the green masses of the thicket were swaying and cracking as the Beast People came rushing together. One face and then another appeared.

'Don't kill it, Prendick,' cried Moreau. 'Don't kill it!' And I saw him stooping as he pushed through under the fronds of the big ferns.

In another moment he had beaten off the Hyæna-Swine with the handle of his whip, and he and Montgomery were keeping away the excited carnivorous Beast People, and particularly M'ling, from the still quivering body. The Hairy Grey Thing came sniffing at the corpse under my arm. The other animals, in their animal ardour, jostled me to get a nearer view.

'Confound you, Prendick!' said Moreau. 'I wanted him.'

'I'm sorry,' said I, though I was not. 'It was the impulse of the moment.' I felt sick with exertion and excitement. Turning, I pushed my way out of the crowding Beast People, and went on alone up the slope towards the higher part of the headland. Under the shouted instructions of Moreau, I heard the three white-swathed Bull Men begin dragging the victim down towards the water.

It was easy now for me to be alone. The Beast People manifested a quite human curiosity about the dead body, and followed it in a thick knot, sniffing and growling at it, as the Bull Men dragged it down the beach. I went to the headland, and watched the Bull Men, black against the evening sky, as they carried the weighted dead body out to sea, and, like a wave across my mind, came the realisation of the unspeakable aimlessness of things upon the island. Upon the beach, among the rocks beneath me, was the Ape Man, the Hyæna-Swine, and several other of the Beast People, standing about Montgomery and Moreau. They were all still intensely excited, and all overflowing with noisy expressions of their loyalty to the Law. Yet I felt an absolute assurance in my own mind that the Hyæna-Swine was implicated in the rabbit-killing. A strange persuasion came upon me that, save for the grossness of the line, the grotesqueness of the forms, I had here before me the whole balance of human life in miniature, the whole interplay of instinct, reason, and fate, in its simplest form. The Leopard Man had happened to go under. That was all the difference.

Poor brutes! I began to see the viler aspect of Moreau's cruelty. I had not thought before of the pain and trouble that came to these poor victims after they had passed from Moreau's hands. I had shivered only at the days of actual torment in the enclosure. But now that seemed to be the lesser part. Before they had been beasts, their instincts fitly adapted to their surroundings, and happy as living things may be. Now they stumbled in the shackles of humanity, lived in a fear that never died, fretted by a law they could not understand; their mock-human existence began in an agony, was one long internal struggle, one long dread of Moreau—and for what? It was the wantonness that stirred me.

Had Moreau had any intelligible object I could have sympathised at least a little with him. I am not so squeamish about pain as that. I could have forgiven him a little even had his motive been hate. But he was so irresponsible, so utterly careless. His curiosity, his mad, aimless investigations, drove him on, and the things were thrown out to live a year or so, to struggle, and blunder, and suffer; at last to die painfully. They were wretched in themselves, the old animal hate moved them to trouble one another; the Law held them back from a brief hot struggle and a decisive end to their natural animosities.

In those days my fear of the Beast People went the way of my personal fear for Moreau. I fell indeed into a morbid state, deep and enduring, alien to fear, which has left permanent scars upon my mind. I must confess I lost faith in the sanity of the world when I saw it suffering the painful disorder of this island. A blind fate, a vast pitiless mechanism, seemed to cut and shape the fabric of existence, and I, Moreau (by his passion for research), Montgomery (by his passion for drink), the Beast People, with their instincts and mental restrictions, were torn and crushed, ruthlessly, inevitably, amid the infinite complexity of its incessant wheels. But this condition did not come all at once. . . . I think indeed that I anticipate a little in speaking of it now.

XVII

A CATASTROPHE

SCARCELY six weeks passed before I had lost every feeling but dislike and abhorrence for these infamous experiments of Moreau's. My one idea was to get away from these horrible caricatures of my Maker's image, back to the sweet and wholesome intercourse of men. My fellow-creatures, from whom I was thus separated, began to assume idyllic virtue and beauty in my memory. My first friendship with Montgomery did not increase. His long separation from humanity, his secret vice of drunkenness, his evident sympathy with the Beast People, tainted him to me. Several times I let him go alone among them. I avoided intercourse with them in every possible way. I spent an increasing proportion of my time upon the beach, looking for some liberating sail that never appeared, until one day there fell upon us an appalling disaster, that put an altogether different aspect upon my strange surroundings.

It was about seven or eight weeks after my landing—rather more, I think, though I had not troubled to keep account of the time—when this catastrophe occurred. It happened in the early morning—I should think about six. I had risen and breakfasted early, having been aroused by the noise of three Beast Men carrying wood into the enclosure.

After breakfast I went to the open gateway of the enclosure and stood there smoking a cigarette and enjoying the freshness of the early morning. Moreau presently came round the corner of the enclosure and greeted me. He passed by me, and I heard him behind me unlock and enter his laboratory. So indurated* was I at that time to the abomination of the place, that I heard without a touch of emotion the puma victim begin another day of torture. It met its persecutor with a shriek almost exactly like that of an angry virago.

Then suddenly something happened. I do not know what it was exactly to this day. I heard a sharp cry behind me, a fall, and turning, saw an awful face rushing upon me, not human, not animal, but hellish, brown, seamed with red branching scars, red drops starting out upon it, and the lidless eyes ablaze. I flung up my arm to defend myself from the blow that flung me headlong with a broken forearm, and the great monster, swathed in lint and with red-stained bandages fluttering about it, leapt over me and passed. I rolled over and over down the beach, tried to sit up, and collapsed upon my broken arm. Then Moreau appeared, his massive white face all the more terrible for the blood that trickled from his forehead. He carried a revolver in one hand. He scarcely glanced at me, but rushed off at once in pursuit of the puma.

I tried the other arm and sat up. The muffled figure in front ran in great striding leaps along the beach, and Moreau followed her. She turned her head and saw him, then, doubling abruptly, made for the bushes. She gained upon him at every stride. I saw her plunge into them, and Moreau, running slantingly to intercept her, fired and missed as she disappeared. Then he too vanished in the green confusion.

I stared after them, and then the pain in my arm flamed up, and with a groan I staggered to my feet. Montgomery appeared in the doorway dressed, and with his revolver in his hand.

'Great God, Prendick!' he said, not noticing that I was hurt. 'That brute's loose! Tore the fetter out of the wall. Have you seen them?' Then sharply, seeing I gripped my arm, 'What's the matter?'

'I was standing in the doorway,' said I.

He came forward and took my arm. 'Blood on the sleeve,' said he, and rolled back the flannel. He pocketed the weapon, felt my arm about painfully, and led me inside. 'Your arm is broken,' he said; and then, 'Tell me exactly how it happened—what happened.'

I told him what I had seen, told him in broken sentences, with gasps of pain between them, and very dexterously and swiftly he bound my arm meanwhile. He slung it from my shoulder, stood back, and looked at me. 'You'll do,' he said. 'And now?' He thought. Then he went out and locked the gates of the enclosure. He was absent some time.

I was chiefly concerned about my arm. The incident seemed merely one more of many horrible things. I sat down in the deck chair and, I must admit, swore heartily at the island. The first dull feeling of injury in my arm had already given way to a burning pain when Montgomery re-appeared.

His face was rather pale, and he showed more of his lower gums than ever. 'I can neither see nor hear anything of him,' he said. 'I've been thinking he may want my help.' He stared at me with his expressionless eyes. 'That was a strong brute,' he said. 'It simply wrenched its fetter out of the wall.'

He went to the window, then to the door, and there turned to me. 'I shall go after him,' he said. 'There's another revolver I can leave with you. To tell you the truth, I feel anxious somehow.'

He obtained the weapon, and put it ready to my hand on the table, then went out, leaving a restless contagion in the air. I did not sit long after he left. I took the revolver in hand and went to the doorway.

The morning was as still as death. Not a whisper of wind was stirring, the sea was like polished glass, the sky empty, the beach desolate. In my half-excited, half-feverish state this stillness of things oppressed me.

I tried to whistle, and the tune died away. I swore again—the second time that morning. Then I went to the corner of the enclosure and stared inland at the green bush that had swallowed up Moreau and Montgomery. When would they return. And how?

Then far away up the beach a little grey Beast Man appeared, ran down to the water's edge, and began splashing about. I strolled back to the doorway, then to the corner again, and so began pacing to and fro like a sentinel upon duty. Once I was arrested by the distant voice of Montgomery bawling, 'Coo-ee . . . Mor-eau!' My arm became less painful, but very hot. I got feverish and thirsty. My shadow grew shorter. I watched the distant figure until it went away again. Would Moreau and Montgomery never return? Three sea-birds began fighting for some stranded treasure.

Then from far away behind the enclosure I heard a pistol-shot. A long silence, and then came another. Then a yelling cry nearer, and another dismal gap of silence. My unfortunate imagination set to work to torment me. Then suddenly a shot close by.

I went to the corner, startled, and saw Montgomery, his face scarlet, his hair disordered, and the knee of his trousers torn. His face expressed profound consternation. Behind him slouched the Beast Man M'ling, and round M'ling's jaws were some ominous brown stains.

'Has he come?' he said.

'Moreau?' said I. 'No.'

'My God!' The man was panting, almost sobbing for breath. 'Go back in,' he said, taking my arm. 'They're mad. They're all rushing about mad. What can have happened? I don't know. I'll tell you when my breath comes. Where's some brandy?'

He limped before me into the room and sat down in the deck chair. M'ling flung himself down just outside the doorway, and began panting like a dog. I got Montgomery some brandy and water. He sat staring blankly in front of him, recovering his breath. After some minutes he began to tell me what had happened.

He had followed their track for some way. It was plain enough at first on account of the crushed and broken bushes, white rags torn from the puma's bandages, and occasional smears of blood on the leaves of the shrubs and undergrowth. He lost the track, however, on the stony ground beyond the stream where I had seen the Beast Man drinking, and went wandering aimlessly westward shouting Moreau's name. Then M'ling had come to him carrying a light hatchet. M'ling had seen nothing of the puma affair, had been felling wood and heard him calling. They went on shouting together. Two Beast Men came crouching and peering at them through the undergrowth, with gestures and a furtive carriage that alarmed Montgomery by their strangeness. He hailed them, and they fled guiltily. He stopped shouting after that, and after wandering some time further in an undecided way, determined to visit the huts.

He found the ravine deserted.

Growing more alarmed every minute, he began to retrace his steps. Then it was he encountered the two Swine Men I had seen dancing on the night of my arrival; blood-stained they were about the mouth, and intensely excited. They came crashing through the ferns, and stopped with fierce faces when they saw him. He cracked his whip in some trepidation, and forthwith they rushed at him. Never before had a Beast Man dared to do that. One he shot through the head, M'ling flung himself upon the other, and the two rolled grappling. M'ling got his brute under and with his teeth in its throat, and Montgomery shot that too as it struggled in M'ling's grip. He had some difficulty in inducing M'ling to come on with him.

Thence they had hurried back to me. On the way M'ling had suddenly rushed into a thicket and driven out an under-sized Ocelot Man, also blood-stained, and lame through a wound in the foot. This brute had run a little way and then turned savagely at bay, and Montgomery—with a certain wantonness I thought—had shot him.

'What does it all mean?' said I.

He shook his head and turned once more to the brandy.

XVIII

THE FINDING OF MOREAU

WHEN I saw Montgomery swallow a third dose of brandy I took it upon myself to interfere. He was already more than half-fuddled. I told him that some serious thing must have happened to Moreau by this time, or he would have returned, and that it behoved us to ascertain what that catastrophe was. Montgomery raised some feeble objections, and at last agreed. We had some food, and then all three of us started.

It is possibly due to the tension of my mind at the time, but even now that start into the hot stillness of the tropical afternoon is a singularly vivid impression. M'ling went first, his shoulders hunched, his strange black head moving with quick starts as he peered first on this side of the way and then on that. He was unarmed. His axe he had dropped when he encountered the Swine Men. Teeth were *his* weapons when it came to fighting. Montgomery followed with stumbling footsteps, his hands in his pockets, his face downcast; he was in a state of muddled sullenness with me on account of the brandy. My left arm was in a sling—it was lucky it was my left,—and I carried my revolver in my right.

We took a narrow path through the wild luxuriance of the island, going north-westward. And presently M'ling stopped and became rigid with watchfulness. Montgomery almost staggered into him, and then stopped too. Then, listening intently, we heard, coming through the trees, the sound of voices, and footsteps approaching us.

'He is dead,' said a deep vibrating voice.

'He is not dead, he is not dead,' jabbered another.

'We saw, we saw,' said several voices.

'*Hul*-lo!' suddenly shouted Montgomery. 'Hullo, there!'

'Confound you!' said I, and gripped my pistol.

There was a silence, then a crashing among the interlacing vegetation, first here, then there, and then half a dozen faces appeared, strange faces, lit by a strange light. M'ling made a growling noise in his throat. I recognised the Ape Man—I had, indeed, already identified his voice—and two of the white-swathed brown-featured creatures I had seen in Montgomery's boat. With them were the two dappled brutes, and that grey horribly crooked creature who said the Law, with grey hair streaming down its cheeks, heavy grey eyebrows, and grey locks pouring off from a central parting upon its sloping forehead, a heavy faceless thing, with strange red eyes, looking at us curiously from amidst the green.

For a space no one spoke. Then Montgomery hiccoughed, 'Who . . . said he was dead?'

The Monkey Man looked guiltily at the Hairy Grey Thing. 'He is dead,' said this monster. 'They saw.'

There was nothing threatening about this detachment at any rate. They seemed awe-stricken and puzzled. 'Where is he?' said Montgomery.

'Beyond,' and the grey creature pointed.

'Is there a Law now?' asked the Monkey Man. 'Is it still to be this and that? Is he dead indeed?' 'Is there a Law?' repeated the man in white. 'Is there a Law, thou Other with the whip? He is dead,' said the Hairy Grey Thing. And they all stood watching us.

'Prendick,' said Montgomery, turning his dull eyes to me. 'He's dead—evidently.'

I had been standing behind him during this colloquy. I began to see how things lay with them. I suddenly stepped in front of him and lifted up my voice:—'Children of the Law,' I said, 'he is *not* dead.'

M'ling turned his sharp eyes on me. 'He has changed his shape—he has changed his body,' I went on. 'For a time you will not see him. He is . . . there,'—I pointed upward—'where he can watch you. You cannot see him. But he can see you. Fear the Law!'

I looked at them squarely. They flinched.

'He is great, he is good,' said the Ape Man, peering fearfully upward among the dense trees.

'And the other Thing?' I demanded.

'The Thing that bled and ran screaming and sobbing—that is dead too,' said the Grey Thing, still regarding me.

'That's well,' grunted Montgomery.

'The Other with the whip,' began the Grey Thing.

'Well?' said I.

'Said he was dead.'

But Montgomery was still sober enough to understand my motive in denying Moreau's death. 'He is not dead,' he said slowly. 'Not dead at all. No more dead than me.'

'Some,' said I, 'have broken the Law. They will die. Some have died. Show us now where his old body lies. The body he cast away because he had no more need of it.'

'It is this way, Man who walked in the Sea,' said the Grey Thing.

And with these six creatures guiding us, we went through the tumult of ferns and creepers and tree-stems towards the north-west. Then came a yelling, a crashing among the branches, and a little pink homunculus rushed by us shrieking. Immediately after appeared a feral monster in headlong pursuit, blood-bedabbled, who was amongst us almost before he could stop his career. The Grey Thing leapt aside; M'ling with a snarl flew at it, and was struck aside; Montgomery fired and missed, bowed his head, threw up his arm, and turned to run. I fired, and the thing still came on; fired again point-blank into its ugly face. I saw its features vanish in a flash. Its face was driven in. Yet it passed me, gripped Montgomery, and holding him, fell headlong beside him, and pulled him sprawling upon itself—in its death-agony.

I found myself alone with M'ling, the dead brute, and the prostrate man. Montgomery raised himself slowly and stared in a muddled way at the shattered Beast Man beside him. It more than half-sobered him. He scrambled to his feet. Then I saw the Grey Thing returning cautiously through the trees.

'See,' said I, pointing to the dead brute. 'Is the Law not alive? This came of breaking the Law.'

He peered at the body. 'He sends the Fire that kills,' said he in his deep voice, repeating part of the ritual.

The others gathered round and stared for a space.

At last we drew near the westward extremity of the island. We came upon the gnawed and mutilated body of the puma, its shoulder-bone smashed by a bullet, and perhaps twenty yards further found at last what we sought. He lay face downward in a trampled space in a cane brake. One hand was almost severed at the wrist, and his silvery hair was dabbled in blood. His head had been battered in by the fetters of the puma. The broken canes beneath him were smeared with blood. His revolver we could not find. Montgomery turned him over.

* * * *

Resting at intervals, and with the help of the seven Beast People—for he was a heavy man,—we carried him back to the enclosure. The night was darkling. Twice we heard unseen creatures howling and shrieking past our little band, and once the little pink sloth creature appeared and stared at us, and vanished again. But we were not attacked again. At the gates of the enclosure our company of Beast People left us—M'ling going with the rest. We locked ourselves in, and then took Moreau's mangled body into the yard, and laid it upon a pile of brushwood.

Then we went into the laboratory and put an end to all we found living there.

XIX

WHEN this was accomplished, and we had washed and eaten, Montgomery and I went into my little room and seriously discussed our position for the first time. It was then near midnight. He was almost sober, but greatly disturbed in his mind. He had been strangely under the influence of Moreau's personality. I do not think it had ever occurred to him that Moreau could die. This disaster was the sudden collapse of the habits that had become part of his nature in the ten or more monotonous years he had spent on the island. He talked vaguely, answered my questions crookedly, wandered into general questions.

'This silly ass of a world,' he said. 'What a muddle it all is! I haven't had any life. I wonder when it's going to begin. Sixteen years being bullied by nurses and schoolmasters at their own sweet will, five in London grinding hard at medicine—bad food, shabby lodgings, shabby clothes, shabby vice—a blunder—*I* didn't know any better—and hustled off to this beastly island. Ten years here! What's it all for, Prendick? Are we bubbles blown by a baby?'

It was hard to deal with such ravings. 'The thing we have to think of now,' said I, 'is how to get away from this island.'

'What's the good of getting away? I'm an outcast. Where am *I* to join on? It's all very well for *you*, Prendick. Poor old Moreau! We can't leave him here to have his bones picked. As it is . . . And besides, what will become of the decent part of the Beast Folk?'

'Well,' said I. 'That will do to-morrow. I've been thinking we might make the brushwood into a pyre and burn his body—and those other things . . . Then what will happen with the Beast Folk?'

'*I* don't know. I suppose those that were made of beasts of prey will make silly asses of themselves sooner or later. We can't massacre the lot. Can we? I suppose that's what *your* humanity would suggest? . . . But they'll change. They are sure to change.'

He talked thus inconclusively until at last I felt my temper going. 'Damnation!' he exclaimed, at some petulance of mine. 'Can't you see I'm in a worse hole than you are?' And he got up and went for the brandy. 'Drink,' he said, returning. 'You logic-chopping, chalky-faced saint of an atheist, drink.'

'Not I,' said I, and sat grimly watching his face under the yellow paraffin flare as he drank himself into a garrulous misery. I have a memory of infinite tedium. He wandered into a maudlin defence of the Beast People and of M'ling. M'ling, he said, was the only thing that had ever really cared for him. And suddenly an idea came to him.

'I'm damned!' said he, staggering to his feet, and clutching the brandy-bottle. By some flash of intuition I knew what it was he intended. 'You don't give drink to that beast!' I said, rising and facing him.

'Beast!' said he. 'You're the beast. He takes his liquor like a Christian. Come out of the way, Prendick.'

'For God's sake,' said I.

'*Get* . . . out of the way,' he roared, and suddenly whipped out his revolver.

'Very well,' said I, and stood aside, half-minded to fall upon him as he put his hand upon the latch, but deterred by the thought of my useless arm. 'You've made a beast of yourself. To the beasts you may go.'

He flung the doorway open and stood, half-facing me, between the yellow lamp-light and the pallid glare of the moon; his eye-sockets were blotches of black under his stubbly eyebrows. 'You're a solemn prig, Prendick, a silly ass! You're always fearing and fancying. We're on the edge of things. I'm bound to cut my throat to-morrow. I'm going to have a damned good bank holiday to-night.'

He turned and went out into the moonlight. 'M'ling,' he cried; 'M'ling, old friend!'

Three dim creatures in the silvery light came along the edge of the wan beach, one a white-wrapped creature, the other two blotches of blackness following it. They halted, staring. Then I saw M'ling's hunched shoulders as he came round the corner of the house.

'Drink,' cried Montgomery; 'drink, ye brutes! Drink, and be men. Dammy, I'm the cleverest! Moreau forgot this. This is the last touch. Drink, I tell you.' And waving the bottle in his hand, he started off at a kind of quick trot to the westward, M'ling ranging himself between him and the three dim creatures who followed.

I went to the doorway. They were already indistinct in the mist of the moonlight before Montgomery halted. I saw him administer a dose of the raw brandy to M'ling, and saw the five figures melt into one vague patch. 'Sing,' I heard Montgomery shout; 'sing all together, "Confound old Prendick." . . . That's right. Now, again: "Confound old Prendick."'

The black group broke up into five separate figures and wound slowly away from me along the band of shining beach. Each went howling at his own sweet will, yelping insults at me, or giving whatever other vent this new inspiration of brandy demanded.

Presently I heard Montgomery's remote voice shouting, 'Right turn!' and they passed with their shouts and howls into the blackness of the landward trees. Slowly, very slowly, they receded into silence.

The peaceful splendour of the night healed again. The moon was now past the meridian and travelling down the west. It was at its full, and very bright, riding through the empty blue sky. The shadow of the wall lay, a yard wide, and of inky blackness, at my feet. The eastward sea was a featureless grey, dark and mysterious, and between the sea and the shadow the grey sands (of volcanic glass and crystals), flashed and shone like a beach of diamonds. Behind me the paraffin lamp flared hot and ruddy.

Then I shut the door, locked it, and went into the enclosure where Moreau lay beside his latest victims—the staghounds and the llama, and some other wretched brutes,—his massive face, calm even after his terrible death, and with the hard eyes open, staring at the dead white moon above. I sat down upon the edge of the sink, and, with my eyes upon that ghastly pile of silvery light and ominous shadows, began to turn over my plans in my mind.

In the morning I would gather some provisions in the dingey, and after setting fire to the pyre before me, push out into the desolation of the high sea once more. I felt that for Montgomery there was no help; that he was in truth half akin to these Beast Folk, unfitted for human kindred. I do not know how long I sat there scheming. It must have been an hour or so. Then my planning was interrupted by the return of Montgomery to my neighbourhood. I heard a yelling from many throats, a tumult of exultant cries, passing down towards the beach, whooping and howling and excited shrieks, that seemed to come to a stop near the water's edge. The riot rose and fell; I heard heavy blows and the splintering smash of wood, but it did not trouble me then. A discordant chanting began.

My thoughts went back to my means of escape. I got up, brought the lamp, and went into a shed to look at some kegs I had seen there. Then I became interested in the contents of some biscuit tins, and opened one. I saw something out of the tail of my eye, a red figure, and turned sharply.

Behind me lay the yard, vividly black and white in the moonlight, and the pile of wood and fagots on which Moreau and his mutilated victims lay, one on another. They seemed to be gripping one another in one last revengeful grapple. His wounds gaped black as night, and the blood that had dripped lay in black patches upon the sand. Then I saw, without understanding, the cause of the phantom, a ruddy glow that came and danced and went upon the wall opposite. I misinterpreted this, fancied it was a reflection of my flickering lamp, and turned again to the stores in the shed. I went on rummaging among them as well as a one-armed man could, finding this convenient thing and that, and putting them aside for to-morrow's launch. My movements were slow, and the time passed quickly. Presently the daylight crept upon me.

The chanting died down, gave place to a clamour, then began again, and suddenly broke into a tumult. I heard cries of 'More, more!' a sound like quarrelling, and a sudden wild shriek. The quality of the sounds changed so greatly that it arrested my attention. I went out into the yard and listened. Then, cutting like a knife across the confusion, came the crack of a revolver.

I rushed at once through my room to the little doorway. As I did so I heard some of the packing-cases behind me go sliding down and smash together, with a clatter of glass on the floor of the shed. But I did not heed these. I flung the door open and looked out.

Up the beach by the boathouse a bonfire was burning, raining up sparks into the indistinctness of the dawn. Around this struggled a mass of black figures. I heard Montgomery call my name. I began to run at once towards this fire, revolver in hand. I saw the pink tongue of Montgomery's pistol lick out once, close to the ground. He was down. I shouted with all my strength and fired into the air.

I heard some one cry 'The Master!' The knotted black struggle broke into scattering units, the fire leapt and sank down. The crowd of Beast People fled in sudden panic before me up the beach. In my excitement I fired at their retreating backs as they disappeared among the bushes. Then I turned to the black heaps upon the ground.

Montgomery lay on his back with the hairy grey Beast Man sprawling across his body. The brute was dead, but still gripping Montgomery's throat with its curving claws. Near by lay M'ling on his face, and quite still, his neck bitten open, and the upper part of the smashed brandy-bottle in his hand. Two other figures lay near the fire, the one motionless, the other groaning fitfully, every now and then raising its head slowly, then dropping it again.

I caught hold of the Grey Man and pulled him off Montgomery's body; his claws drew down the torn coat reluctantly as I dragged him away.

Montgomery was dark in the face and scarcely breathing. I splashed sea-water on his face, and pillowed his head on my rolled-up coat. M'ling was dead. The wounded creature by the fire—it was a Wolf Brute with a bearded grey face—lay, I found, with the fore part of its body upon the still glowing timber. The wretched thing was injured so dreadfully that in mercy I blew its brains out at once. The other brute was one of the Bull Men swathed in white. He too was dead.

The rest of the Beast People had vanished from the beach. I went to Montgomery again and knelt beside him, cursing my ignorance of medicine.

The fire beside me had sunk down, and only charred beams of timber glowing at the central ends, and mixed with a grey ash of brushwood, remained. I wondered casually where Montgomery had got his wood. Then I saw that the dawn was upon us. The sky had grown brighter, the setting moon was growing pale and opaque in the luminous blue of the day. The sky to the eastward was rimmed with red.

Then I heard a thud and a hissing behind me, and, looking round, sprang to my feet with a cry of horror. Against the warm dawn great tumultuous masses of black smoke were boiling up out of the enclosure, and through their stormy darkness shot flickering threads of blood-red flame. Then the thatched roof caught. I saw the curving charge of the flames across the sloping straw. A spurt of fire jetted from the window of my room.

I knew at once what had happened. I remembered the crash I had heard. When I had rushed out to Montgomery's assistance I had overturned the lamp.

The hopelessness of saving any of the contents of the enclosure stared me in the face. My mind came back to my plan of flight, and turning swiftly I looked to see where the two boats lay upon the beach. They were gone! Two axes lay upon the sands beside me, chips and splinters were scattered broadcast, and the ashes of the bonfire were blackening and smoking under the dawn. He had burnt the boats to revenge himself upon me and prevent our return to mankind.

A sudden convulsion of rage shook me. I was almost moved to batter his foolish head in as he lay there helpless at my feet. Then suddenly his hand moved, so feebly, so pitifully, that my wrath vanished. He groaned and opened his eyes for a minute.

I knelt down beside him and raised his head. He opened his eyes again, staring silently at the dawn, and then they met mine. The lids fell. 'Sorry,' he said presently, with an effort. He seemed trying to think. 'The last,' he murmured, 'the last of this silly universe. What a mess——'

I listened. His head fell helplessly to one side. I thought some drink might revive him, but there was neither drink nor vessel in which to bring drink at hand. He seemed suddenly heavier. My heart went cold.

I bent down to his face, put my hand through the rent in his blouse. He was dead; and even as he died a line of white heat, the limb of the sun, rose eastward beyond the projection of the bay, splashing its radiance across the sky, and turning the dark sea into a weltering tumult of dazzling light. It fell like a glory upon his death-shrunken face.

I let his head fall gently upon the rough pillow I had made for him, and stood up. Before me was the glittering desolation of the sea, the awful solitude upon which I had already suffered so much; behind me the island, hushed under the dawn, its Beast People silent and unseen. The enclosure with all its provisions and ammunition burnt noisily, with sudden gusts of flame, a fitful crackling, and now and then a crash. The heavy smoke drove up the beach away from me, rolling low over the distant tree-tops towards the huts in the ravine. Beside me were the charred vestiges of the boats and these five dead bodies.

Then out of the bushes came three Beast People, with hunched shoulders, protruding heads, misshapen hands awkwardly held, and inquisitive unfriendly eyes, and advanced towards me with hesitating gestures.

XX

ALONE WITH THE BEAST FOLK

I FACED these people, facing my fate in them, single-handed—now literally single-handed, for I had a broken arm. In my pocket was a revolver with two empty chambers. Among the chips scattered about the beach lay the two axes that had been used to chop up the boats. The tide was creeping in behind me.

There was nothing for it but courage. I looked squarely into the faces of the advancing monsters. They avoided my eyes, and their quivering nostrils investigated the bodies that lay beyond me on the beach. I took half a dozen steps, picked up the blood-stained whip that lay beneath the body of the Wolf Man, and cracked it.

They stopped and stared at me. 'Salute,' said I. 'Bow down!'

They hesitated. One bent his knees. I repeated my command, with my heart in my mouth, and advanced upon them. One knelt, then the other two.

I turned and walked towards the dead bodies, keeping my face towards the three kneeling Beast Men, very much as an actor passing up the stage faces his audience.

'They broke the Law,' said I, putting my foot on the Sayer of the Law. 'They have been slain. Even the Sayer of the Law. Even the Other with the whip. Great is the Law! Come and see.'

'None escape,' said one of them, advancing and peering.

'None escape,' said I. 'Therefore hear and do as I command.' They stood up, looking questioningly at one another.

'Stand there,' said I.

I picked up the hatchets and swung them by their heads from the sling of my arm, turned Montgomery over, picked up his revolver, still loaded in two chambers, and bending down to rummage, found half a dozen cartridges in his pocket.

'Take him,' said I, standing up again and pointing with the whip; 'take him and carry him out, and cast him into the sea.'

They came forward, evidently still afraid of Montgomery, but still more afraid of my cracking red whip-lash, and, after some fumbling and hesitation, some whip-cracking and shouting, lifted him gingerly, carried him down to the beach, and went splashing into the dazzling welter of the sea. 'On,' said I, 'on!—carry him far.'

They went in up to their armpits and stood regarding me. 'Let go,' said I, and the body of Montgomery vanished with a splash. Something seemed to tighten across my chest. 'Good!' said I, with a break in my voice, and they came back, hurrying and fearful, to the margin of the water, leaving long wakes of black in the silver. At the water's edge they stopped, turning and glaring into the sea as though they presently expected Montgomery to arise thencefrom and exact vengeance.

'Now these,' said I, pointing to the other bodies.

They took care not to approach the place where they had thrown Montgomery into the water, but, instead, carried the four dead Beast People slantingly along the beach for perhaps a hundred yards before they waded out and cast them away.

As I watched them disposing of the mangled remains of M'ling I heard a light footfall behind me, and turning quickly saw the big Hyæna-Swine perhaps a dozen yards away. His head was bent down, his bright eyes were fixed upon me, his stumpy hands clenched and held close by his side. He stopped in this crouching attitude when I turned, his eyes a little averted.

For a moment we stood eye to eye. I dropped the whip and snatched at the pistol in my pocket. For I meant to kill this brute—the most formidable of any left now upon the island—at the first excuse. It may seem treacherous, but so I was resolved. I was far more afraid of him than of any other two of the Beast Folk. His continued life was, I knew, a threat against mine.

I was perhaps a dozen seconds collecting myself. Then I cried, 'Salute! Bow down!'

His teeth flashed upon me in a snarl. 'Who are *you*, that I should. . . .'

Perhaps a little too spasmodically, I drew my revolver, aimed, and quickly fired. I heard him yelp, saw him run sideways and turn, knew I had missed, and clicked back the cock with my thumb for the next shot. But he was already running headlong, jumping from side to side, and I dared not risk another miss. Every now and then he looked back at me over his shoulder. He went slanting along the beach, and vanished beneath the driving masses of dense smoke that were still pouring out from the burning enclosure. For some time I stood staring after him. I turned to my three obedient Beast Folk again, and signalled them to drop the body they still carried. Then I went back to the place by the fire where the bodies had fallen, and kicked the sand until all the brown blood-stains were absorbed and hidden.

I dismissed my three serfs with a wave of the hand, and went up the beach into the thickets. I carried my pistol in my hand, my whip thrust, with the hatchets, in the sling of my arm. I was anxious to be alone, to think out the position in which I was now placed.

A dreadful thing, that I was only beginning to realise, was that over all this island there was now no safe place where I could be alone, and secure to rest or sleep. I had recovered strength amazingly since my landing, but I was still inclined to be nervous, and to break down under any great stress. I felt I ought to cross the island, and establish myself with the Beast People, making myself secure in their confidence. And my heart failed me. I went back to the beach, and, turning eastward past the burning enclosure, made for a point where a shallow spit of coral sand ran out towards the reef. Here I could sit down and think, my back to the sea, and my face against any surprise. And there I sat, chin on knees, the sun beating down upon my head, and a growing dread in my mind, plotting how I could live on against the hour of my rescue (if ever rescue came). I tried to review the whole situation as calmly as I could, but it was impossible to clear the thing of emotion.

I began turning over in my mind the reason of Montgomery's despair. 'They will change,' he said. 'They are sure to change.' And Moreau—what was it that Moreau had said? 'The stubborn beast flesh grows day by day back again. . . .' Then I came round to the Hyæna-Swine. I felt assured that if I did not kill that brute he would kill me. . . . The Sayer of the Law was dead—worse luck! . . . They knew now that we of the Whips could be killed, even as they themselves were killed. . . .

Were they peering at me already out of the green masses of ferns and palms over yonder—watching until I came within their spring? Were they plotting against me? What was the Hyæna-Swine telling them? My imagination was running away with me into a morass of unsubstantial fears.

My thoughts were disturbed by a crying of sea-birds, hurrying towards some black object that had been stranded by the waves on the beach near the enclosure. I knew what that object was, but I had not the heart to go back and drive them off. I began walking along the beach in the opposite direction, designing to come round the eastward corner of the island, and so approach the ravine of the huts, without traversing the possible ambuscades of the thickets.

Perhaps half a mile along the beach I became aware of one of my three Beast Folk advancing out of the landward bushes towards me. I was now so nervous with my own imaginings that I immediately drew my revolver. Even the propitiatory gestures of the creature failed to disarm me.

He hesitated as he approached. 'Go away!' cried I. There was something very suggestive of a dog in the cringing attitude of the creature. It retreated a little way, very like a dog being sent home, and stopped, looking at me imploringly with canine brown eyes. 'Go away,' said I. 'Do not come near me.'

'May I not come near you?' it said.

'No. Go away,' I insisted, and snapped my whip. Then, putting my whip in my teeth, I stooped for a stone, and with that threat drove the creature away.

So, in solitude, I came round by the ravine of the Beast People, and, hiding among the weeds and reeds that separated this crevice from the sea, I watched such of them as appeared, trying to judge from their gestures and appearance how the death of Moreau and Montgomery and the destruction of the House of Pain had affected them. I know now the folly of my cowardice. Had I kept my courage up to the level of the dawn, had I not allowed it to ebb away in solitary thought, I might have grasped the vacant sceptre of Moreau, and ruled over the Beast People. As it was, I lost the opportunity, and sank to the position of a mere leader among my fellows.

Towards noon certain of them came and squatted basking in the hot sand. The imperious voices of hunger and thirst prevailed over my dread. I came out of the bushes, and, revolver in hand, walked down towards these seated figures. One, a Wolf Woman, turned her head and stared at me, and then the others. None attempted to rise or salute me. I felt too faint and weary to insist against so many, and I let the moment pass.

'I want food,' said I, almost apologetically, and drawing near.

'There is food in the huts,' said an Ox-Boar Man drowsily, and looking away from me.

I passed them, and went down into the shadow and odours of the almost deserted ravine. In an empty hut I feasted on some specked and half-decayed fruit, and then, after I had propped some branches and sticks about the opening,* and placed myself with my face towards it, and my hand upon my revolver, the exhaustion of the last thirty hours claimed its own, and I let myself fall into a light slumber, trusting that the flimsy barricade I had erected would cause sufficient noise in its removal to save me from surprise.

XXI

THE REVERSION OF THE BEAST FOLK

IN this way I became one among the Beast People in the Island of
Doctor Moreau. When I awoke it was dark about me. My arm ached
in its bandages. I sat up, wondering at first where I might be. I heard
coarse voices talking outside. Then I saw that my barricade had gone,
and that the opening of the hut stood clear. My revolver was still in
my hand.

I heard something breathing, saw something crouched together
close beside me. I held my breath, trying to see what it was. It began
to move slowly, interminably. Then something soft and warm and moist
passed across my hand.

All my muscles contracted. I snatched my hand away. A cry of alarm
began, and was stifled in my throat. Then I just realised what had
happened sufficiently to stay my fingers on the revolver.

'Who is that?' I said in a hoarse whisper, the revolver still pointed.

'*I*, Master.'

'Who are you?'

'They say there is no Master now. But I know, I know. I carried the
bodies into the sea, O Walker in the Sea, the bodies of those you slew.
I am your slave, Master.'

'Are you the one I met on the beach?' I asked.

'The same, Master.'

The thing was evidently faithful enough, for it might have fallen
upon me as I slept. 'It is well,' I said, extending my hand for another
licking kiss. I began to realise what its presence meant, and the tide of
my courage flowed. 'Where are the others?' I asked.

'They are mad. They are fools,' said the Dog Man. 'Even now they
talk together beyond there. They say, "The Master is dead; the Other
with the Whip is dead. That Other who walked in the Sea is—as we
are. We have no Master, no Whips, no House of Pain any more. There is
an end. We love the Law, and will keep it; but there is no pain, no Master,
no Whips for ever again." So they say. But I know, Master, I know.'

I felt in the darkness and patted the Dog Man's head. 'It is well,'
I said again.

'Presently you will slay them all,' said the Dog Man.

'Presently,' I answered, 'I will slay them all—after certain days and certain things have come to pass. Every one of them save those you spare, every one of them shall be slain.'

'What the Master wishes to kill the Master kills,' said the Dog Man with a certain satisfaction in his voice.

'And that their sins may grow,' I said; 'let them live in their folly until their time is ripe. Let them not know that I am the Master.'

'The Master's will is sweet,' said the Dog Man, with the ready tact of his canine blood.

'But one has sinned,' said I. 'Him I will kill, whenever I may meet him. When I say to you, "*That is he*," see that you fall upon him.—And now I will go to the men and women who are assembled together.'

For a moment the opening of the hut was blackened by the exit of the Dog Man. Then I followed and stood up, almost in the exact spot where I had been when I had heard Moreau and his staghound pursuing me. But now it was night, and all the miasmatic ravine about me was black, and beyond, instead of a green sunlit slope, I saw a red fire before which hunched grotesque figures moved to and fro. Further were the thick trees, a bank of black fringed above with the black lace of the upper branches. The moon was just riding up on the edge of the ravine, and like a bar across its face drove the spire of vapour that was for ever streaming from the fumarolles of the island.

'Walk by me,' said I, nerving myself, and side by side we walked down the narrow way, taking little heed of the dim things that peered at us out of the huts.

None about the fire attempted to salute me. Most of them disregarded me—ostentatiously. I looked round for the Hyæna-Swine, but he was not there. Altogether, perhaps, twenty of the Beast Folk squatted, staring into the fire or talking to one another.

'He is dead, he is dead, the Master is dead,' said the voice of the Ape Man to the right of me. 'The House of Pain—there *is* no House of Pain.'

'He is not dead,' said I, in a loud voice. 'Even now he watches us.'

This startled them. Twenty pairs of eyes regarded me.

'The House of Pain is gone,' said I. 'It will come again. The Master you cannot see. Yet even now he listens above you.'

'True, true!' said the Dog Man.

They were staggered at my assurance. An animal may be ferocious and cunning enough, but it takes a real man to tell a lie. 'The Man with the Bandaged Arm speaks a strange thing,' said one of the Beast Folk.

'I tell you it is so,' I said. 'The Master and the House of Pain will come again. Woe be to him who breaks the Law!'

They looked curiously at one another. With an affectation of indifference I began to chop idly at the ground in front of me with my hatchet. They looked, I noticed, at the deep cuts I made in the turf.

Then the Satyr raised a doubt; I answered him, and then one of the dappled things objected, and an animated discussion sprang up round the fire. Every moment I began to feel more convinced of my present security. I talked now without the catching in my breath, due to the intensity of my excitement, that had troubled me at first. In the course of about an hour I had really convinced several of the Beast Folk of the truth of my assertions, and talked most of the others into a dubious state. I kept a sharp eye for my enemy the Hyæna-Swine, but he never appeared. Every now and then a suspicious movement would startle me, but my confidence grew rapidly. Then as the moon crept down from the zenith, one by one the listeners began to yawn (showing the oddest teeth in the light of the sinking fire), and first one, and then another, retired towards the dens in the ravine. And I, dreading the silence and darkness, went with them, knowing I was safer with several of them than with one alone.

In this manner began the longer part of my sojourn upon this Island of Doctor Moreau. But from that night until the end came there was but one thing happened to tell, save a series of innumerable small unpleasant details and the fretting of an incessant uneasiness. So that I prefer to make no chronicle for that gap of time, to tell only one cardinal incident of the ten months I spent as an intimate of these half-humanised brutes. There is much that sticks in my memory that I could write, things that I would cheerfully give my right hand to forget. But they do not help the telling of the story. In the retrospect it is strange to remember how soon I fell in with these monsters' ways and gained my confidence again. I had my quarrels, of course, and could show some teeth-marks still, but they soon gained a wholesome respect for my trick of throwing stones and the bite of my hatchet. And my St Bernard Dog Man's loyalty was of infinite service to me. I found their simple scale of honour was based mainly on the capacity for inflicting trenchant wounds. Indeed I may say—without vanity, I hope—that I held something like a pre-eminence among them. One or two whom, in various disputes, I had scarred rather badly, bore me a grudge, but it vented itself, chiefly behind my back, and at a safe distance from my missiles, in grimaces.

The Hyæna-Swine avoided me, and I was always on the alert for him. My inseparable Dog Man hated and dreaded him intensely. I really believe that was at the root of the brute's attachment to me. It was soon evident to me that the former monster had tasted blood, and gone the way of the Leopard Man. He formed a lair somewhere in the forest, and became solitary. Once I tried to induce the Beast Folk to hunt him, but I lacked the authority to make them co-operate for one end. Again and again I tried to approach his den and come upon him unawares, but always he was too acute for me, and saw or winded* me and got away. He too made every forest pathway danger-ous to me and my allies with his lurking ambuscades. The Dog Man scarcely dared to leave my side.

In the first month or so the Beast Folk, compared with their latter condition, were human enough, and for one or two besides my canine friend I even conceived a friendly tolerance. The little pink sloth crea-ture displayed an odd affection for me, and took to following me about. The Monkey Man bored me, however. He assumed, on the strength of his five digits, that he was my equal, and was for ever jab-bering at me, jabbering the most arrant nonsense. One thing about him entertained me a little: he had a fantastic trick of coining new words. He had an idea, I believe, that to gabble about names that meant nothing was the proper use of speech. He called it 'big thinks,' to distinguish it from 'little thinks'—the sane everyday interests of life. If ever I made a remark he did not understand, he would praise it very much, ask me to say it again, learn it by heart, and go off repeating it, with a word wrong here or there, to all the milder of the Beast People. He thought nothing of what was plain and comprehensible. I invented some very curious 'big thinks' for his especial use. I think now that he was the silliest creature I ever met; he had developed in the most wonderful way the distinctive silliness of man without losing one jot of the natural folly of a monkey.

This, I say, was in the earlier weeks of my solitude among these brutes. During that time they respected the usage established by the Law, and behaved with general decorum. Once I found another rab-bit torn to pieces—by the Hyæna-Swine, I am assured,—but that was all. It was about May when I first distinctly perceived a growing difference in their speech and carriage, a growing coarseness of articulation, a growing disinclination to talk. My Monkey Man's jabber multiplied in volume, but grew less and less comprehensible, more and more simian. Some of the others seemed altogether slipping their hold upon speech, though they still understood what I said to them at that time. Can you imagine language, once clear-cut and exact, softening and guttering, losing shape and import, becoming mere lumps of sound again? And they walked erect with an increasing difficulty. Though they evidently felt ashamed of themselves, every now and then I would come upon one or other running on toes and finger-tips, and quite unable to recover the vertical attitude. They held things more clumsily; drinking by suction, feeding by gnawing; grew commoner every day. I realised more keenly than ever what Moreau had told me about the 'stubborn beast flesh.' They were reverting, and reverting very rapidly.

Some of them—the pioneers, I noticed with some surprise, were all females—began to disregard the injunction of decency—deliberately for the most part. Others even attempted public outrages upon the institution of monogamy. The tradition of the Law was clearly losing its force. I cannot pursue this disagreeable subject. My Dog Man imperceptibly slipped back to the dog again; day by day he became dumb, quadrupedal, hairy. I scarcely noticed the transition from the companion on my right hand to the lurching dog at my side. As the carelessness and disorganisation increased from day to day, the lane of dwelling places, at no time very sweet, became so loathsome that I left it, and going across the island made myself a hovel of boughs amid the black ruins of Moreau's enclosure. Some memory of pain, I found, still made that place the safest from the Beast Folk.

It would be impossible to detail every step of the lapsing of these monsters; to tell how, day by day, the human semblance left them; how they gave up bandagings and wrappings, abandoned at last every stitch of clothing; how the hair began to spread over the exposed limbs; how their foreheads fell away and their faces projected; how the quasi-human intimacy I had permitted myself with some of them in the first month of my loneliness became a horror to recall.

The change was slow and inevitable. For them and for me it came without any definite shock. I still went among them in safety, because no jolt in the downward glide had released the increasing charge of explosive animalism that ousted the human day by day. But I began to fear that soon now that shock must come. My St Bernard Brute followed me to the enclosure, and his vigilance enabled me to sleep at times in something like peace. The little pink sloth thing became shy and left me, to crawl back to its natural life once more among the tree-branches. We were in just the state of equilibrium that would remain in one of those 'Happy Family' cages that animal-tamers exhibit, if the tamer were to leave it for ever.

Of course these creatures did not decline into such beasts as the reader has seen in zoological gardens—into ordinary bears, wolves, tigers, oxen, swine, and apes. There was still something strange about each; in each Moreau had blended this animal with that; one perhaps was ursine chiefly, another feline chiefly, another bovine chiefly, but each was tainted with other creatures—a kind of generalised animalism appeared through the specific dispositions. And the dwindling shreds of the humanity still startled me every now and then, a momentary recrudescence of speech perhaps, an unexpected dexterity of the forefeet, a pitiful attempt to walk erect.

I too must have undergone strange changes. My clothes hung about me as yellow rags, through whose rents glowed the tanned skin. My hair grew long, and became matted together. I am told that even now my eyes have a strange brightness, a swift alertness of movement.

At first I spent the daylight hours on the southward beach watching for a ship, hoping and praying for a ship. I counted on the *Ipecacuanha* returning as the year wore on, but she never came. Five times I saw sails, and thrice smoke, but nothing ever touched the island. I always had a bonfire ready, but no doubt the volcanic reputation of the island was taken to account for that.

It was only about September or October that I began to think of making a raft. By that time my arm had healed, and both my hands were at my service again. At first I found my helplessness appalling. I had never done any carpentry or suchlike work in my life, and I spent day after day in experimental chopping and binding among the trees. I had no ropes, and could hit on nothing wherewith to make ropes; none of the abundant creepers seemed limber or strong enough, and with all my litter of scientific education I could not devise any way of making them so. I spent more than a fortnight grubbing among the black ruins of the enclosure and on the beach where the boats had been burnt, looking for nails and other stray pieces of metal that might prove of service. Now and then some Beast creature would watch me, and go leaping off when I called to it. There came a season of thunderstorms and heavy rain that greatly retarded my work, but at last the raft was completed.

I was delighted with it. But with a certain lack of practical sense that has always been my bane I had made it a mile or more from the sea, and before I had dragged it down to the beach the thing had fallen to pieces. Perhaps it is as well that I was saved from launching it. But at the time my misery at my failure was so acute, that for some days I simply moped on the beach and stared at the water and thought of death.

But I did not mean to die, and an incident occurred that warned me unmistakably of the folly of letting the days pass so—for each fresh day was fraught with increasing danger from the Beast Monsters. I was lying in the shade of the enclosure wall staring out to sea, when I was startled by something cold touching the skin of my heel, and starting round found the little pink sloth creature blinking into my face. He had long since lost speech and active movement, and the lank hair of the little brute grew thicker every day, and his stumpy claws more askew. He made a moaning noise when he saw he had attracted my attention, went a little way towards the bushes, and looked back at me.

At first I did not understand, but presently it occurred to me that he wished me to follow him, and this I did at last, slowly—for the day was hot. When he reached the trees he clambered into them, for he could travel better among their swinging creepers than on the ground.

And suddenly in a trampled space I came upon a ghastly group. My St Bernard creature lay on the ground dead, and near his body crouched the Hyæna-Swine, gripping the quivering flesh with misshapen claws, gnawing at it and snarling with delight. As I approached the monster lifted its glaring eyes to mine, its lips went trembling back from its red-stained teeth, and it growled menacingly. It was not afraid and not ashamed; the last vestige of the human taint had vanished. I advanced a step further, stopped, pulled out my revolver. At last I had him face to face.

The brute made no sign of retreat. But its ears went back, its hair bristled, and its body crouched together. I aimed between the eyes and fired. As I did so the thing rose straight at me in a leap, and I was knocked over like a ninepin. It clutched at me with its crippled hand,

and struck me in the face. Its spring carried it over me. I fell under the hind part of its body, but luckily I had hit as I meant, and it had died even as it leapt. I crawled out from under its unclean weight and stood up trembling, staring at its quivering body. That danger at least was over. But this, I knew, was only the first of the series of relapses that must come.

I burnt both the bodies on a pyre of brushwood. Now, indeed, I saw clearly that unless I left the island my death was only a question of time. The Beasts by that time had, with one or two exceptions, left the ravine, and made themselves lairs, according to their tastes, among the thickets of the island. Few prowled by day; most of them slept, and the island might have seemed deserted to a newcomer; but at night the air was hideous with their calls and howling. I had half a mind to make a massacre of them—to build traps or fight them with my knife. Had I possessed sufficient cartridges, I should not have hesitated to begin the killing. There could now be scarcely a score left of the dangerous carnivores; the braver of these were already dead. After the death of this poor dog of mine, my last friend, I too adopted to some extent the practice of slumbering in the daytime, in order to be on my guard at night. I rebuilt my den in the walls of the enclosure with such a narrow opening that anything attempting to enter must necessarily make a considerable noise. The creatures had lost the art of fire, too, and recovered their fear of it. I turned once more, almost passionately now, to hammering together stakes and branches to form a raft for my escape.

I found a thousand difficulties. I am an extremely unhandy man— my schooling was over before the days of Slöjd,*—but most of the requirements of a raft I met at last in some clumsy circuitous way or other, and this time I took care of the strength. The only insurmountable obstacle was, that I had no vessel to contain the water I should need if I floated forth upon these untravelled seas. I would have even tried pottery, but the island contained no clay. I used to go moping about the island, trying with all my might to solve this one last difficulty. Sometimes I would give way to wild outbursts of rage, and hack and splinter some unlucky tree in my intolerable vexation. But I could think of nothing.

And then came a day, a wonderful day, that I spent in ecstasy. I saw a sail to the southwest, a small sail like that of a little schooner, and forthwith I lit a great pile of brushwood and stood by it in the heat of it and the heat of the midday sun, watching. All day I watched that sail, eating or drinking nothing, so that my head reeled; and the Beasts came and glared at me, and seemed to wonder, and went away. The boat was still distant when night came and swallowed it up, and all night I toiled to keep my blaze bright and high, and the eyes of the Beasts shone out of the darkness, marvelling. In the dawn it was nearer, and I saw it was the dirty lug-sail of a small boat. My eyes were weary with watching, and I peered and could not believe them. Two men were in the boat, sitting low down, one by the bows, the other at the rudder. But the boat sailed strangely. The head was not kept to the wind; it yawed* and fell away.

As the day grew brighter I began waving the last rag of my jacket to them; but they did not notice me, and sat still, facing one another. I went to the lowest point of the low headland and gesticulated and shouted. There was no response, and the boat kept on her aimless course, making slowly, very slowly, for the bay. Suddenly a great white bird flew up out of the boat, and neither of the men stirred nor noticed it. It circled round, and then came sweeping overhead with its strong wings outspread.

Then I stopped shouting, and sat down on the headland and rested my chin on my hands and stared. Slowly, slowly, the boat drove past towards the west. I would have swum out to it, but something, a cold vague fear, kept me back. In the afternoon the tide stranded it, and left it a hundred yards or so to the westward of the ruins of the enclosure.

The men in it were dead, had been dead so long that they fell to pieces when I tilted the boat on its side and dragged them out. One had a shock of red hair like the captain of the *Ipecacuanha*, and a dirty white cap lay in the bottom of the boat. As I stood beside the boat, three of the Beasts came slinking out of the bushes and sniffing towards me. One of my spasms of disgust came upon me. I thrust the little boat down the beach and clambered on board her. Two of the brutes were Wolf Beasts, and came forward with quivering nostrils and glittering eyes; the third was the horrible nondescript of bear and bull.

When I saw them approaching those wretched remains, heard them snarling at one another, and caught the gleam of their teeth, a frantic horror succeeded my repulsion. I turned my back upon them, struck the lug, and began paddling out to sea. I could not bring myself to look behind me.

But I lay between the reef and the island that night, and the next morning went round to the stream and filled the empty keg aboard with water. Then, with such patience as I could command, I collected a quantity of fruit, and waylaid and killed two rabbits with my last three cartridges. While I was doing this I left the boat moored to an inward projection of the reef, for fear of the Beast Monsters.

XXII

THE MAN ALONE

In the evening I started and drove out to sea before a gentle wind from the south-west, slowly and steadily, and the island grew smaller and smaller, and the lank spire of smoke dwindled to a finer and finer line against the hot sunset. The ocean rose up around me, hiding that low dark patch from my eyes. The daylight, the trailing glory of the sun, went streaming out of the sky, was drawn aside like some luminous curtain, and at last I looked into that blue gulf of immensity that the sunshine hides, and saw the floating hosts of the stars. The sea was silent, the sky was silent; I was alone with the night and silence.

So I drifted for three days, eating and drinking sparingly, and meditating upon all that had happened to me,* nor desiring very greatly then to see men again. One unclean rag was about me, my hair a black tangle. No doubt my discoverers thought me a madman. It is strange, but I felt no desire to return to mankind. I was only glad to be quit of the foulness of the Beast Monsters. And on the third day I was picked up by a brig from Apia* to San Francisco. Neither the captain nor the mate would believe my story, judging that solitude and danger had made me mad. And fearing their opinion might be that of others, I refrained from telling my adventure further, and professed to recall nothing that had happened to me between the loss of the *Lady Vain* and the time when I was picked up again—the space of a year.

I had to act with the utmost circumspection to save myself from the suspicion of insanity. My memory of the Law, of the two dead sailors, of the ambuscades of the darkness, of the body in the cane brake, haunted me. And, unnatural as it seems, with my return to mankind came, instead of that confidence and sympathy I had expected, a strange enhancement of the uncertainty and dread I had experienced during my stay upon the island. No one would believe me, I was almost as queer to men as I had been to the Beast People. I may have caught something of the natural wildness of my companions.

They say that terror is a disease, and anyhow, I can witness that, for several years now, a restless fear has dwelt in my mind, such a restless fear as a half-tamed lion cub may feel. My trouble took the strangest form. I could not persuade myself that the men and women I met were not also another, still passably human, Beast People, animals half-wrought into the outward image of human souls, and that they would presently begin to revert, to show first this bestial mark and then that. But I have confided my case to a strangely able man, a man who had known Moreau, and seemed half to credit my story, a mental specialist—and he has helped me mightily.

Though I do not expect that the terror of that island will ever altogether leave me, at most times it lies far in the back of my mind, a mere distant cloud, a memory and a faint distrust; but there are times when the little cloud spreads until it obscures the whole sky. Then I look about me at my fellow-men. And I go in fear. I see faces keen and bright, others dull or dangerous, others unsteady, insincere; none that have the calm authority of a reasonable soul. I feel as though the animal was surging up through them; that presently the degradation of the Islanders will be played over again on a larger scale. I know this is an illusion, that these seeming men and women about me are indeed men and women, men and women for ever, perfectly reasonable creatures, full of human desires and tender solicitude, emancipated from instinct, and the slaves of no fantastic Law—beings altogether different from the Beast Folk. Yet I shrink from them, from their curious glances, their inquiries and assistance, and long to be away from them and alone.

For that reason I live near the broad free downland, and can escape thither when this shadow is over my soul; and very sweet is the empty downland then, under the wind-swept sky. When I lived in London the horror was wellnigh insupportable. I could not get away from men; their voices came through windows; locked doors were flimsy safeguards. I would go out into the streets to fight with my delusion, and prowling women would mew after me, furtive craving men glance jealously at me, weary pale workers go coughing by me, with tired eyes and eager paces like wounded deer dripping blood, old people, bent and dull, pass murmuring to themselves, and all unheeding a ragged tail of gibing children. Then I would turn aside into some chapel, and even there, such was my disturbance, it seemed that the preacher gibbered Big Thinks even as the Ape Man had done; or into some library, and there the intent faces over the books seemed but patient creatures waiting for prey. Particularly nauseous were the blank, expressionless faces of people in trains and omnibuses; they seemed no more my fellow-creatures than dead bodies would be, so that I did not dare to travel unless I was assured of being alone. And even it seemed that I, too, was not a reasonable creature, but only an animal tormented with some strange disorder in its brain, that sent it to wander alone, like a sheep stricken with gid.*

But this is a mood that comes to me now—I thank God—more rarely. I have withdrawn myself from the confusion of cities and multitudes, and spend my days surrounded by wise books, bright windows in this life of ours lit by the shining souls of men. I see few strangers, and have but a small household. My days I devote to reading and to experiments in chemistry, and I spend many of the clear nights in the study of astronomy. There is, though I do not know how there is or why there is, a sense of infinite peace and protection in the glittering hosts of heaven. There it must be, I think, in the vast and eternal laws of matter, and not in the daily cares and sins and troubles of men, that whatever is more than animal within us must find its solace and its hope. I hope, or I could not live. And so, in hope and solitude, my story ends.

EDWARD PRENDICK.*

NOTE.*—The substance of the chapter entitled 'Dr Moreau Explains,' which contains the essential idea of the story, appeared as a middle article in the *Saturday Review* in January 1895. This is the only portion of this story that has been previously published, and it has been entirely recast to adapt it to the narrative form. Strange as it may seem to the unscientific reader, there can be no denying that, whatever amount of credibility attaches to the detail of this story, the manufacture of monsters—and perhaps even of *quasi*-human monsters—is within the possibilities of vivisection.

EXPLANATORY NOTES

ABBREVIATIONS

Atlantic	*The Works of H. G. Wells*, Atlantic Edition, 24 vols. (London: T. Fisher Unwin, 1924). *The Island of Doctor Moreau* is in volume ii.
EB	*Encyclopædia Britannica*
Heinemann 1896	H. G. Wells, *The Island of Doctor Moreau* (London: William Heinemann, 1913). First edition of the novel, on which this text is based.
Heinemann 1913	H. G. Wells, *The Island of Doctor Moreau* (London: William Heinemann, 1913). Revised edition, with many changes from first edition; provided the textual basis for Atlantic *Moreau*.
OED	*Oxford English Dictionary*
Penguin	H. G. Wells, *The Island of Doctor Moreau*, ed. Patrick Parrinder with an introduction by Margaret Atwood and notes by Steven McLean (London: Penguin, 2005).
S&K	H. G. Wells, *The Island of Doctor Moreau* (New York: Stone and Kimball, 1896). First American edition.

3 *INTRODUCTION*: this section does not appear in Atlantic.

latitude 1° s. and longitude 107° w.: the *Lady Vain* sinks in the Pacific Ocean, significantly due west of the Galapagos Islands off the coast of Peru. Charles Darwin visited the Galapagos in 1835, as part of the voyage of HMS *Beagle*, and the archipelago's unique wildlife proved a major inspiration for his formulation of the theory of natural selection.

Callao: major port city on the coast of Peru.

latitude 5° 3′ s. and longitude 101° w.: in the Pacific Ocean, some 600 miles south-west of the Galapagos.

schooner Ipecacuanha: a schooner is 'A small sea-going fore-and-aft rigged vessel, originally with only two masts, but now often with three or four masts and carrying one or more topsails' (*OED*). Ipecacuanha is a flowering plant native to South America, with psychotropic and emetic qualities— thus appropriate to the novel's tone of hallucinatory disgust.

latitude 5° s. and longitude 105° w.: the longitude of '105° E' in Heinemann 1896 is an obvious error which was later corrected to 105° w. for Heinemann 1913. These coordinates are close to the Galapagos.

Arica: port city in northern Chile. S&K has 'Africa' here.

copra: dried coconut, specifically for use in the production of coconut oil.

Banya: unclear. There are a number of Banyas and Banias, largely in Bulgaria, none of which is near the sea.

7 *Medusa case*: in 1816, the French frigate *Méduse* ran aground and sank. The ship's lifeboats proved inadequate to tow the 147 survivors to safety, so they were cast adrift on an improvised raft. Thirteen days later, the raft was rescued with only fifteen survivors, who had resorted to murder and cannibalism. The episode was immortalized in Théodore Gericault's great painting, *The Raft of the Medusa* (1818–19).

gig: 'A light, narrow, clinker-built ship's boat, adapted either for rowing or sailing' (*OED*).

bowsprit: 'A large spar or boom running out from the stem of a vessel, to which (and the jib-boom and flying jib-boom, which extend beyond it) the foremast stays are fastened' (*OED*).

breaker: a small keg or cask. Atlantic reads 'a small beaker of water' here, an incorrect (though understandable) transcription of the first edition.

8 *the thing we all had in mind*: cannibalism. See Introduction, pp. xxix–xxx.

we handed halfpence: we drew lots.

thwarts: a seat on a rowing boat, where the rower sits.

10 *gunwale*: the upper edge of a ship's side.

she certainly acts according: that is, the *Ipecacuanha*, named after an emetic plant (see note to p. 3), sways and makes those on board seasick.

11 *I did my Biology at University College*: Montgomery's education is similar to Prendick's, and to HGW's, who studied biology under T. H. Huxley at the Normal School of Science, now Imperial College (see note to p. 26). University College London, founded in 1826, is based in Bloomsbury, central London.

radula: 'The movable rasping structure in the mouth of many molluscs, bearing chitinous teeth and used for scraping off and drawing in food particles' (*OED*).

Tottenham Court Road and Gower Street: Tottenham Court Road is a major thoroughfare in central London. Gower Street, in Bloomsbury, runs parallel to it and is the main location of University College London.

Caplatzi: A. Caplatzi sold scientific apparatus at 3 Chenies Street, which runs between Tottenham Court Road and Gower Street.

12 *scuttle*: a small hole in the deck or side of a ship.

duck things: sailors' garments made of linen.

13 *companion*: a frame or opening leading from the quarterdeck to the cabins below.

hatchway: an opening in the ship's deck, through which cargo is lowered to the hold.

14 *staghounds*: deer hounds, very large hunting dogs.

mizzen: the mizzenmast is the rear mast of a ship, aft (behind) the main mast.

bulwark: raised woodwork along the sides of a ship, running above the deck.

spankers: a spanker is 'A fore-and-aft sail, set with a gaff and boom at the aftermost part of the ship' (*OED*).

taffrail: rail at the very back (aft) of a ship.

15 *forecastle*: a short raised deck at the very front (fore) of a ship; pronounced fo'c'sle.

main shrouds: a pair of ropes leading down from the main mast, forming part of a ship's rigging.

hazed: beaten.

pertinacious: obstinate.

16 *the law and the prophets*: Matt. 7:12: 'Therefore all things whatsoever ye would that men should do to you, do ye even so to them: for this is the law and the prophets.'

17 *hove to*: came to a standstill.

binnacle lantern: the binnacle is the box on deck in which the ship's compass is placed.

20 *THE MAN WHO HAD NOWHERE TO GO*: in Atlantic, this chapter is entitled 'The Landing on the Island', perhaps to avoid confusion with Chapter II: 'The Man Who Was Going Nowhere'.

mizzen spanker boom: a spar running out from the mizzenmast (see note to p. 14), to which is affixed the spanker sail (see note to p. 14).

the whole bilin' of 'em: 'the whole boiling of them'; the whole lot of them.

21 *dumbfounded*: Heinemann 1896 has 'dumfounded', a spelling error corrected for Atlantic and subsequent editions.

lugs: lug-sails; four-cornered sails.

22 *heeling*: the leaning of a ship to one side in the water.

24 *painter*: a short rope attached to the front of a small boat, for tying it to the quay or to a ship.

piggin: a wooden pail or drinking vessel.

25 *pumiceous lava*: pumice stone; porous and light volcanic rock.

26 *Royal College of Science . . . Huxley*: the Royal College of Science is the Normal School of Science, now Imperial College London. T. H. Huxley (1825–95), major English evolutionary biologist, was the dean of the Royal College of Science from 1881. Prendick's education is thus exactly the same as HGW's own.

28 *Bluebeard's Chamber*: Bluebeard is a serial wife-murderer, who locks his victims' corpses in a forbidden chamber in his castle. He first appeared in Charles Perrault's *Contes de ma mère l'oye* (*Tales of Mother Goose*, 1697), and has featured in many subsequent versions of the tale.

29 *languages I cannot read with any comfort*: like HGW, Prendick has not had a classical education.

30 *transfusion of blood*: the beneficial possibilities of blood transfusion were realized across the nineteenth century, but were without firm scientific basis until Karl Landsteiner's discovery of human blood groups in 1901.

31 *silly season*: the summer months, during the parliamentary recess, when newspapers generally resorted to publishing trivial stories in the absence of political news.

halitus: 'A vapour, exhalation' (*OED*).

vivisection: scientific experimentation upon live subjects. See Introduction, pp. xxv–xxvii.

33 *Horace*: Quintus Horatius Flaccus (65–8 BC), Latin poet; best known for his Odes and for the work of poetic theory *Ars Poetica* (*The Art of Poetry*, *c.* 19 BC).

35 *epiphyte*: a plant which grows (but does not feed) on another plant.

36 *foliaceous lichen, but deliquescing into slime*: foliaceous means leafy or leaf-like; deliquescing means melting away, or becoming liquid.

37 *heavy chinless faces, retreating foreheads*: here and elsewhere, the physiognomy of HGW's beast men strongly resembles that of the congenitally criminal 'types' identified by the influential Italian criminologist Cesare Lombroso (1835–1909), in works such as *L'uomo delinquante* (1876; translated into English as *Criminal Man*, 1911). For a study of the influence of physiognomy on the nineteenth-century novel, see Lucy Hartley, *Physiognomy and the Meaning of Expression in Nineteenth-Century Culture* (Cambridge, 2001).

38 *mark of the beast*: see Revelation 13:16–18:

> And he causeth all, both small and great, rich and poor, free and bond, to receive a mark in their right hand, or in their foreheads:
> And that no man might buy or sell, save he that had the mark, or the name of the beast, or the number of his name.
> Here is wisdom. Let him that hath understanding count the number of the beast: for it is the number of a man; and his number *is* Six hundred threescore *and* six.

'The Mark of the Beast' is the title of an important colonial horror story by Rudyard Kipling, first published in 1890, and with strong resonance for *The Island of Doctor Moreau*. In Kipling's tale, a British colonial official desecrates a Hindu altar, and is punished by being transformed into a rabid leopard man.

40 *the yellow brilliance of the evening star*: the planet Venus, which shines a distinct pale yellow when it appears in the evening sky.

44 *bogle*: a phantom, often as here used dismissively to mean 'A thing unsubstantial, a mere phantom' (*OED*).

45 *carbolic acid*: phenol, extracted from coal tar; an important component in the manufacture of plastics, but also with numerous pharmaceutical uses, including as a detergent and an antiseptic.

46 *Comus rout*: in John Milton's masque *Comus* (1634), Comus, the son of Bacchus and Circe, offers a thirst-quenching potion to sailors, which transforms them

> Into some brutish form of wolf or bear,
> Or ounce or tiger, hog or bearded goat,
> All other parts remaining as they were.

HGW seems to be alluding here to Sir Edwin Landseer's painting *The Defeat of Comus* (1843), which was circulated in a popular engraving as *The Rout of Comus and His Band*, and which contains vivid and disturbing renditions of a variety of Beast People.

49 *scoriæ*: 'Rough clinker-like masses formed by the cooling of the surface of molten lava upon exposure to the air, and distended by the expansion of imprisoned gases' (*OED*).

52 *'Not to go on all-Fours . . . Are we not Men?'*: HGW conceived of *Moreau* as 'a theological grotesque' (Atlantic, vol. ii, p. ix), as is particularly evident in the biblical cadences of this passage. The novel's perceived blasphemy proved understandably controversial, and resulted in some hostile reviews: see Introduction, pp. xxvii–xxviii.

Flesh nor Fish: Heinemann 1913 has 'Flesh or Fish'; Atlantic has 'Flesh of Fish'.

53 *Skye terrier*: a breed of small dog native to Britain, and characterized by a distinctive long, straight coat which falls over the face and eyes, and often covers the legs like a cloth.

56 *the haha of an English park*: a ha-ha is a sunken fence or ditch, particularly characteristic of English landscape gardens, where it separates the tended gardens from the pastureland beyond without interrupting the line of sight in the way that a wall would.

58 *slight Pacific tide*: unlike the Atlantic Ocean, whose tides are semidiurnal (twice daily), Pacific tides are generally diurnal (daily), and characterized by small tidal ranges (*EB*).

60 *Hi non sunt homines . . . vivisected*: bad schoolboy Latin for 'They are not men. They are animals which we have . . . vivisected.'

63 *Hunter's cockspur . . . flourished on the bull's neck*: John Hunter (1728–93); surgeon and anatomist, whose collection formed the basis of the Hunterian Museum in the Royal College of Surgeons, London. Hunter was a pioneer of modern vivisection, and performed a number of transplant and grafting operations on live subjects.

rhinoceros rats of the Algerian zouaves: zouaves were 'a body of light infantry in the French army, originally recruited from the Algerian Kabyle tribe of Zouaoua' (*OED*). HGW's source here appears to be Francis T. Buckland's *Curiosities of Natural History* (1858), 125–6: 'the Zouaves perform the Hunterian experiment of transplanting one part of an animal's body on to another. . . . The "trumpet-rat" is modern; its existence dates from the time the Zouaves were in Africa. . . . [I]t is a rat which has a trumpet . . . on his nose like a rhinoceros.'

63 *L'Homme qui Rit*: Victor Hugo's *L'Homme qui rit* (*The Man Who Laughs*, 1869), whose hero is disfigured with a permanent grin, contains an account of the Comprachicos ('child-buyers'), who have 'a genius for disfigurement': 'The Comprachicos worked on man as the Chinese work on trees. . . . A sort of fantastic stunted thing left their hands; it was ridiculous and wonderful': Hugo, *Works*, vi. *The Man Who Laughs, Claude Gueux* (Boston: Jefferson, n.d.), 25.

64 *the Siamese Twins*: conjoined twins; a specific reference to the original 'Siamese Twins', Chang and Eng Bunker (1811–74). Born in Mekong, Thailand (then Siam), the twins initially became famous touring the world as anatomical exhibitions in the 1830s, before settling down to married life (to the sisters Adeline and Sarah Anne Yates) as naturalized American citizens in North Carolina.

65 *You are a materialist*: following the publication of Darwin's *On the Origin of Species* in 1859, the debate over scientific materialism (or scientific naturalism) was one of the most controversial of the latter nineteenth century. Particularly prevalent from the 1870s onwards, and with T. H. Huxley as a prominent voice, scientific materialism completely rejected any metaphysical basis for existence.

66 *houri*: 'a beautiful maiden who awaits the devout Muslim in paradise' (*EB*).

the mark of the beast: see note to p. 38.

the extreme limit of plasticity in a living shape: Moreau's account in this chapter draws heavily on one of Wells's scientific articles, 'The Limits of Individual Plasticity', *Saturday Review* 79 (19 January 1895), 89–90. Wells's article asks why heredity should be the only governing factor in morphology, and speculates as to whether human science can intervene in the evolutionary process: 'a living being may be regarded as something plastic, something that may be shaped and altered, . . . taken in hand and so moulded and modified that at best it would retain scarcely anything of its inherent form and disposition'.

Kanakas: South Sea Islanders.

67 *a fair specimen of the negroid type*: *Dr Moreau* is in part influenced by nineteenth-century racial theory, established in works such as Arthur, comte de Gobineau's *Essay on the Inequality of the Human Races* (1853–5). Josiah C. Nott and George Gliddon's *Types of Mankind* (1854) drew explicit connections between 'negroid' people and apes, and was an influential text in the establishment of the theory of polygeny (multiple births), which maintained that each of the races was separately created (and thus did not share a common ancestor or need be understood as equal). See Introduction, pp. xxx–xxxi.

68 *the stubborn beast flesh*: Heinemann 1896 has 'the stubborn beast flash', an obvious error (in what may be the novel's most famous line), corrected for subsequent editions.

72 *fumarolles*: a fumarole is 'A hole or vent through which vapour issues from a volcano; a smoke-hole' (*OED*).

acquired human characteristics: the inheritance of acquired characteristics is a major element of the influential evolutionary thinking of the French naturalist Jean-Baptiste Lamarck (1744–1829). Lamarckian evolution was superseded and disproved by Darwinian natural selection (and later by genetics). Thus, Moreau practises 'mad science' not only because of his lack of ethics but also because of his adherence to outmoded theories.

73 *prognathous*: having a large, projecting jaw.

74 *fusees*: large-headed matches, also known as lucifers or vesuvians.

76 *the coarser Hebrew type . . . Satanic*: another example of the influence of nineteenth-century racial theory, or 'scientific racism', upon the novel: see note to p. 67.

77 *'Ollendorffian beggar!'*: Heinrich Gottfried Ollendorff (1803–65), German grammarian and language educator; a pioneering figure in the teaching of foreign languages, and author of *Oral System of Teaching Living Languages* (1834), as well as a number of foreign-language grammars. Montgomery is insulting the Satyr for his stilted English.

78 *ambuscades*: ambushes.

84 *others of its pursuers*: Heinemann 1896 has 'other of its pursuers', a mistake repeated in Heinemann 1913, and in Atlantic. Penguin corrects this grammatical error to 'others of its pursuers'.

86 *indurated*: hardened.

104 *In an empty hut . . . about the opening*: Heinemann 1896 reads 'In an empty hut I feasted on some fruit, and then after I had propped some specked and half-decayed branches about the opening', an obvious mistake immediately corrected in S&K, though reappearing in Heinemann 1913 and in Atlantic.

108 *winded*: sniffed, got wind of.

112 *Slöjd*: sloyd; a system of woodwork teaching introduced to Britain in the 1880s. The name derives from the Swedish for 'handicrafts'.

113 *yawed*: steered away from its course.

115 *all that had happened to me*: Heinemann 1896 and Atlantic have 'all that happened to me'; S&K and Penguin have 'all that had happened to me', which is probably more correct.

Apia: the capital of Samoa.

117 *gid*: from 'giddiness'—a fatal brain-disease of sheep, characterized by unsteadiness and loss of balance.

EDWARD PRENDICK: this name at the end does not appear in Atlantic.

118 *NOTE*: this does not appear in Atlantic.

The Oxford World's Classics Website

www.worldsclassics.co.uk

- Browse the full range of Oxford World's Classics online
- Sign up for our monthly e-alert to receive information on new titles
- Read extracts from the Introductions
- Listen to our editors and translators talk about the world's greatest literature with our Oxford World's Classics audio guides
- Join the conversation, follow us on Twitter at OWC_Oxford
- Teachers and lecturers can order inspection copies quickly and simply via our website

www.worldsclassics.co.uk

American Literature

British and Irish Literature

Children's Literature

Classics and Ancient Literature

Colonial Literature

Eastern Literature

European Literature

Gothic Literature

History

Medieval Literature

Oxford English Drama

Philosophy

Poetry

Politics

Religion

The Oxford Shakespeare

A complete list of Oxford World's Classics, including Authors in Context, Oxford English Drama, and the Oxford Shakespeare, is available in the UK from the Marketing Services Department, Oxford University Press, Great Clarendon Street, Oxford OX2 6DP, or visit the website at www.oup.com/uk/worldsclassics.

In the USA, visit www.oup.com/us/owc for a complete title list.

Oxford World's Classics are available from all good bookshops. In case of difficulty, customers in the UK should contact Oxford University Press Bookshop, 116 High Street, Oxford OX1 4BR.

	Late Victorian Gothic Tales
	Literature and Science in the Nineteenth Century
JANE AUSTEN	**Emma**
	Mansfield Park
	Persuasion
	Pride and Prejudice
	Selected Letters
	Sense and Sensibility
MRS BEETON	**Book of Household Management**
MARY ELIZABETH BRADDON	**Lady Audley's Secret**
ANNE BRONTË	**The Tenant of Wildfell Hall**
CHARLOTTE BRONTË	**Jane Eyre**
	Shirley
	Villette
EMILY BRONTË	**Wuthering Heights**
ROBERT BROWNING	**The Major Works**
JOHN CLARE	**The Major Works**
SAMUEL TAYLOR COLERIDGE	**The Major Works**
WILKIE COLLINS	**The Moonstone**
	No Name
	The Woman in White
CHARLES DARWIN	**The Origin of Species**
THOMAS DE QUINCEY	**The Confessions of an English Opium-Eater**
	On Murder
CHARLES DICKENS	**The Adventures of Oliver Twist**
	Barnaby Rudge
	Bleak House
	David Copperfield
	Great Expectations
	Nicholas Nickleby

ANTHONY TROLLOPE

The American Senator
An Autobiography
Barchester Towers
Can You Forgive Her?
Cousin Henry
Doctor Thorne
The Duke's Children
The Eustace Diamonds
Framley Parsonage
He Knew He Was Right
Lady Anna
The Last Chronicle of Barset
Orley Farm
Phineas Finn
Phineas Redux
The Prime Minister
Rachel Ray
The Small House at Allington
The Warden
The Way We Live Now

ANTON CHEKHOV

About Love and Other Stories
Early Stories
Five Plays
The Princess and Other Stories
The Russian Master and Other Stories
The Steppe and Other Stories
Twelve Plays
Ward Number Six and Other Stories

FYODOR DOSTOEVSKY

Crime and Punishment
Devils
A Gentle Creature and Other Stories
The Idiot
The Karamazov Brothers
Memoirs from the House of the Dead
Notes from the Underground and
    The Gambler

NIKOLAI GOGOL

Dead Souls
Plays and Petersburg Tales

MIKHAIL LERMONTOV

A Hero of Our Time

ALEXANDER PUSHKIN

Boris Godunov
Eugene Onegin
The Queen of Spades and Other Stories

LEO TOLSTOY

Anna Karenina
The Kreutzer Sonata and Other Stories
The Raid and Other Stories
Resurrection
War and Peace

IVAN TURGENEV

Fathers and Sons
First Love and Other Stories
A Month in the Country

	French Decadent Tales
	Six French Poets of the Nineteenth Century
HONORÉ DE BALZAC	**Cousin Bette**
	Eugénie Grandet
	Père Goriot
	The Wild Ass's Skin
CHARLES BAUDELAIRE	**The Flowers of Evil**
	The Prose Poems and Fanfarlo
DENIS DIDEROT	**Jacques the Fatalist**
	The Nun
ALEXANDRE DUMAS (PÈRE)	**The Black Tulip**
	The Count of Monte Cristo
	Louise de la Vallière
	The Man in the Iron Mask
	La Reine Margot
	The Three Musketeers
	Twenty Years After
	The Vicomte de Bragelonne
ALEXANDRE DUMAS (FILS)	**La Dame aux Camélias**
GUSTAVE FLAUBERT	**Madame Bovary**
	A Sentimental Education
	Three Tales
VICTOR HUGO	**Notre-Dame de Paris**
J.-K. HUYSMANS	**Against Nature**
PIERRE CHODERLOS DE LACLOS	**Les Liaisons dangereuses**
MME DE LAFAYETTE	**The Princesse de Clèves**
GUILLAUME DU LORRIS and JEAN DE MEUN	**The Romance of the Rose**